—

NICOLE

I HANG up the phone and breathe a sigh of relief. Clutching my phone to my chest, I turn to my sister and nod.

"I got the job."

"Woohoo!" Jenna jumps up and down. The soapy spatula she was washing drips over the kitchen floor, but she ignores it. "Congratulations! I was sure you'd get it."

"I wasn't." I push the hair off my forehead and blow the air out of my lungs. I slump down at the kitchen table. "Thank God. I'll have enough to pay rent for February."

Jenna slides her arm across my shoulders and hugs me. I wince as pain shoots through my right side, but I try to hide it.

"I'm happy for you, Nicole." Her eyes crinkle as she smiles. "That'll take some pressure off."

"Yeah, now I can replace financial stress with work stress."

"Don't be so pessimistic," she laughs. "Come on. Things are looking up!"

I nod and try to smile. "Yeah, they are." At least I won't have to worry about the debt collectors coming to knock down my door. I'll be able to start making payments on these medical bills—maybe even more than the minimum payment. Paralegal salaries aren't amazing, but they're better than the zero I've been making so far.

"Did she tell you what the salary will be?" Jenna asks, reading my mind. She returns the spatula to the sink and keeps washing.

I nod. "Fifty-two grand a year to start, plus benefits."

Jenna smiles. "I knew this would work out. I can see a light at the end of the tunnel. I'm going to make some tea. You want some?"

"Sure." I force a smile. She must be further ahead of me in this tunnel, because I still don't see any light. I shift in my seat, taking a deep breath as pain shoots through my side. I stand up and take a few steps to try to loosen it up.

"Still sore?" Jenna frowns at me as she fills the kettle.

"Yeah. I ran out of pain medication last week. Once I get paid at this job, I'll get some more, but these next few weeks will be a little rough."

"I'll cover the next batch of medication, Nic. I hate seeing you like this."

I shake my head. "You were just telling me about all the expenses with the kids. I'm not going to be your third child," I grin. "I'll be fine. It's not that bad."

Jenna nods as I walk back and forth to try to ease the aches pulsing through the side of my body. Ever since the accident last year, my whole body has rebelled against me. My sister watches me and shakes her head.

"If I ever find the coward that did this to you, I will kill him myself," she says. "He didn't even stop to see if you guys were okay! Who knows what would have happened if the ambulance had gotten there sooner? Jack might have lived! And don't get me started on the insurance company."

A plate clatters in the sink as Jenna shakes her head.

HATE AT FIRST SIGHT

LOVE/HATE: BOOK 1

LILIAN MONROE

~

If you'd like access to the Lilian Monroe Freebie Central, which includes bonus chapters from all my books (including this one), just follow the link below:

http://www.lilianmonroe.com/subscribe

Lilian
xox

Grief carves out another piece of my heart as I take a deep breath. Jenna's still angry—maybe I would be, too, if this had happened to her. But it happened to me, and mostly I just feel exhausted.

When the car hit us, Jack died instantly. That's what the doctors told us, anyway. My sister doesn't believe them. We were told that my husband and I sat on the side of the road for fifteen to thirty minutes before we were found by another driver. It took another ten minutes for the ambulance to arrive. My injuries were severe, but I was able to keep my life. My back was broken and I had a severe concussion, but I wasn't paralyzed.

I was lucky, the doctors said.

Lucky.

For many dark months after the accident, when I was learning how to walk again, I wondered if Jack got the better bargain. Why would I want to live in a world where he doesn't exist? He was the love of my life, and now he's gone.

Things would be easier if Jack's life insurance policy had paid out by now, but the company keeps stalling. It's been a *year*, and they still haven't accepted my claim. They keep asking me for Jack's medical records over and over. They won't give me a straight answer, and fear gnaws at my stomach. If they try to reject my claim, the future is going to be bleak.

Tears smart in my eyes as I sit down again. Jenna sighs.

"Oh, Nicole, I'm sorry. I got carried away. I just get so mad when I start thinking about it."

"I know."

She puts her hands on her hips. "Look, you'll start working and things will get better. The hospital will stop hassling you when you start making payments. You'll get health insurance with the job. You might even meet a sexy hot-shot lawyer!"

I snort, shaking my head. "Not interested. I never liked the hot-shot lawyers at my last firm. Too full of themselves."

Plus, looking at anyone in a romantic way would feel like I was cheating on Jack.

"Well, maybe there will be another paralegal that you can befriend. You'll get out and start meeting people again! Even if it's just work, it'll be good for you."

"Yeah," I reply, mostly so that she'll stop talking about it. Jenna puts a cup of tea in front of me and sighs. I love my sister, but her eternal optimism is exhausting. I'm in a deep, dark hole that she will never understand.

The front door flies open and the pitter-patter of little feet accompanies the giggles of small children. My niece and nephew, Gabby and Taylor, come tumbling into the kitchen like two bowling balls. Jenna scoops them up and covers them with kisses as they laugh, squirming in her arms. Taylor, the younger one, presents her with a drawing he made in school.

My brother-in-law appears in the doorway. He kisses Jenna and asks about her day. Suddenly, I feel like an intruder in their happy life. When Christian lovingly wraps his arms around Jenna, it feels like I'm suffocating. Every time I look at my sister's happiness, it feels like I'm staring directly at the midday sun. It's blinding.

That used to be *me*. I used to be the one with a happy marriage, a happy life, and a loving husband. We'd been talking about kids, too.

Now all I've got is crushing loneliness and overwhelming medical bills.

And a new job, I guess.

I push myself off my chair, leaving my tea untouched. "I'm

going to head to the pool." I smooth my hands on my jeans, clearing my throat. "Good to see you guys."

"You don't want to stay for dinner?" Jenna asks, surprise etched on her face.

I smile and shake my head. If only she knew how painful that would be for me.

"Got to do my workout. The physio says I've been making great progress."

"Okay." She stares at me with those big, brown, motherly eyes of hers, and all I want to do is run away. She hugs me again, more gently this time. "Taylor! Gabby! Say goodbye to Auntie Nicole."

My niece and nephew leave big, sloppy kisses on my cheeks. Christian waves at me, and I finally escape out the front door. I get to my car and let out a sigh.

Guilt creeps into my heart when I watch them through the window. Jenna has been so supportive, even though her life is hectic. She's always checking up on me and making sure I have everything I need. She's loaned me so much money that it makes my head spin.

And yet, being at her house makes me feel like I'm drowning in my own grief. It makes me feel selfish and ungrateful.

It makes me sad.

I sigh and turn the key in the ignition. I wasn't lying to her, at least. I *am* going to go to the pool, and the physio has been impressed with my progress. So, at least my guilt won't be compounded with a lie. As soon as I turn the corner and put her house behind me, I let my shoulders relax in relief.

2

MARTIN

I LOOK up when there's a knock on the door. Kelly, my assistant, pokes her head in.

"These came for you," she says, lifting a bouquet of flowers. My heart squeezes, and I nod.

"Just put them on the table there," I say, gesturing to the coffee table. My office has a plush seating area next to the bookshelves, and I typically like to keep it clear of clutter. Kelly nods quietly and arranges the flowers before slipping out. I say nothing, turning instead to the stack of papers in front of me.

We have a tough case load at the firm right now, and I'm starting to feel snowed under. I glance at the bouquet of flowers and sigh. I push myself back from my large oak desk and stand up. My legs feel stiff, and I stretch my back out. I'll need to go for a swim or a run tonight—something to loosen up.

First, though, I walk over to the large bouquet of white lilies and pluck the card from the blooms. The scent from the flowers is nauseating. As soon as I smell a lily, my mind zips back to that day one year ago, when my whole world changed.

My condolences, Marty.

— Mom

I sigh, tossing the card aside. I know she's trying to keep the memory of Brianne alive, but all I want to do is forget. Especially today.

The year has been a blur. I went back to work right away and buried myself in case after case. It helps me forget about the lonely house and lonely life that I've been left with. It's not all bad, though. Working so hard means I made partner at one of the biggest law firms in Colorado.

Not bad for a thirty-two-year-old man. When I graduated from law school, I didn't think it would happen so fast.

I didn't think I'd be a thirty-two-year-old widower either, but hey. Things change.

I look at the lilies for a few more moments and feel the armor around my heart harden a little bit more.

I sit down at my desk again and try to focus on the stack of papers in front of me. My eyes keep drifting to the bouquet of flowers, though, and soon I'm grabbing my jacket and heading for the door. I thought I'd made it through today unscathed, and then my mother had to go and be thoughtful. How rude of her.

I grab the vase on the way out. I consider tossing the whole thing in the garbage, but that feels disrespectful. So instead, I put it on the firm's front desk. Brianne would have liked that. She always brightened up a room, and she was always the first person people noticed.

I take a deep breath and turn away from the flowers, heading for the elevator.

I need to get out of here. I need to wash the smell of the lilies off my body and I need to exhaust myself physically so that I can get a couple hours of sleep tonight.

That's what happens when you lose your wife and unborn child. It tends to change a person.

In the aftermath I've been so numb inside that I worked myself to the bone. I made partner at the firm, so it's all worth it, right?

I mash the elevator buttons and sigh. When the doors close and the nauseating stench of lilies dissipates, I breathe a sigh of relief.

WHEN I PULL into the pool parking lot, my shoulders relax. After an hour or so here, my body will be tired enough to shut off my brain. This is my safe place. It's the place where Brianne's memory doesn't invade my thoughts without warning.

It's busy tonight—there must be some group lessons going on. I turn down one aisle of the parking lot just as another car comes toward me. It's an old beat-up Honda Civic, and I can hear from all the way over here that the engine isn't in good shape.

I can tell the Civic is vying for the one free parking space between us.

I don't know if it's work stress, or the flowers, or just the fact that today is today, but anger flares in my chest. That should be my parking space. Not some shitty rust bucket in need of an oil change.

I press on the accelerator, but I'm too late. The car slides into the spot and my rage burns hotter. I roll past slowly, waiting for the parking-space-stealer to show himself.

Someone gets out of the car and I can't help myself. I pull my handbrake and hop out.

"That was my parking space," I call out as I take a step toward the Honda.

The person has their head in the back seat, rummaging around for something. I take a couple steps toward the car, and finally a head pops up above the Honda's rusty old roof.

I almost yelp in surprise. The woman looks exactly like Brianne.

Well, not exactly. She's taller, and her hair is dark brown whereas Brianne's was almost blonde. This woman's lips are fuller.

But it's her eyes.

She arches her eyebrow and looks at me from the other side of her car. Slamming the back door closed, she slings her bag over her shoulder and starts walking toward the back of the car. She looks on the ground and then pokes her head toward the front of her car.

Finally, she turns back to me. I fold my arms across my chest, and her eyes flick to my biceps. I flex—I can't help it.

"Don't see your name on it."

Her voice is like sarcasm dripping in honey. I imagine slamming her against the back of the car and running my hands up between those long legs of hers. I'd teach her a lesson about talking back.

"You know full-well that I was heading for it."

"I didn't even see you until you drove by," she scoffs. She folds her arms over her chest, mimicking my movement. "You think being on the other end of the parking lot entitles you to all the spaces?"

She glances at my car, shaking her head. "Typical BMW driver."

Blood rushes between my legs. My cock is rock hard as I stare at her perfect lips. Her steely grey eyes stare at me, defiant. I'm almost impressed. No one talks to me like this—ever.

"What's that supposed to mean?" I arch my eyebrow, taking a step toward her.

She waves her hand at my car, shaking her head. "You're all entitled pricks."

Shock silences me. Who is this chick?

She stares at me, challenging me to answer. Her long, slender fingers drum on her bicep as she waits for me to say something. I can't though. I'm too busy wondering what those fingers would look like wrapped around my cock.

"As much as I'm enjoying this little staring contest," she says, dropping her arms to her sides, "I've got some swimming to do. Or do you own the whole pool, too?"

"What if I did?" *Great comeback.*

She just rolls her eyes and walks toward the building. My eyes follow her, dropping down to the movement of her ass as she walks away.

"Enjoying the view?" She calls out without turning around.

Anger burns a hole in my chest. Who the fuck does she think she is? I jump back into my car and rage as I find another parking space.

All I wanted to do was come to the pool and swim some laps to cool down. I didn't ask for this! First, she steals my parking space and then she gives me that fucking attitude.

I turn off the car and tighten my hands on the steering wheel. My knuckles turn white as I try to understand what's going on inside me.

Maybe it's just anger and adrenaline. This is just a rage

boner. It's not the way her eyes glided over my body, or the way she walked away from me. It's not the way her voice zipped through my body like a bolt of lightning.

I wish I could bury my cock inside her and fuck the sarcasm right out of her voice. My chest heaves, and I close my eyes.

I'm just mad. I'm stressed about work. I'm stressed about today.

I look down at my crotch and take a deep breath. I squeeze my eyes shut, and all I can see is that sassy, irreverent, foul-mouthed beauty.

When my body has cooled down enough to walk into the building, I grab my bag and stomp toward the entrance... toward *her*.

3

NICOLE

ADRENALINE COURSES through my veins as I near the building. My cheeks feel red and my heart is thumping. I resist the urge to look back at the man.

How dare he come out and accuse me of stealing his parking space? First of all, *who does that*? And second of all, I did no such thing!

I clearly had my turn signal on before he did. I was the first one to get to the parking spot. How could he think he owned it?

Never mind the fact that his eyes were blazing with danger, and his whole body screamed sin. Never mind the fact that his biceps strained against his crisp white shirt. Never mind how he was staring at my body as if he wanted to rip my clothes off right then and there.

And I *liked* it.

No, he was an entitled prick. Nothing more.

Still, when I push the doors open, I can't help but look back at the parking lot. His car is gone from the aisle, but I think I see it in the back corner of the lot. I take a deep breath and step inside.

Dwelling on assholes like that isn't exactly going to help me prepare for my first day of work tomorrow. I should be calming down, not getting in fights over a parking spot. Who am I, George Costanza?

I inhale the scent of chlorine as I walk in. I rummage through my purse and find the swipe card, putting it next to the card reader to walk past the turnstiles.

I swipe it and step forward, like I always do. My legs bang up against the turnstile and I frown. I try swiping the card again but it just flashes red.

"Hi Nicole," the receptionist, Mary, calls out. "Looks like your membership just expired yesterday. I can sign you up for another year, if you want?"

My eyebrows shoot up. Has it been a year already? It feels like I just paid the pool fee last month! I nod, walking over toward the front desk.

"Sure thing, Mary. Here." I hand her the card and look for my wallet. She taps on the computer and smiles at me.

"Did you want to sign up for a full year? It's four hundred for the year, or forty per month if you wanted to go month to month."

My eyebrows shoot up. Four hundred dollars? I hadn't planned for that at all.

I shake my head. "I'll go for the month-to-month for now."

"Are you sure? You're here all the time, and it works out cheaper if you—"

"Month to month is fine." My voice is strained, and I try to cover it up with a thin smile. Mary nods. My hand is shaking as I hand her my credit card. I definitely don't have four hundred dollars before this card is maxed out, but forty should be okay.

She swipes the card just as the front door swings open. I

close my eyes in mortification as the sexy stranger from the parking lot struts through the door. He has a small duffel bag in his hand, and he glances at me as his eyes blaze.

His shirt stretches over his chest, and his perfectly-tailored, expensive-looking pants make him look seven feet tall. Isn't he cold? It's below freezing and he isn't wearing a jacket! His eyebrow arches as our eyes meet, and heat pools in the pit of my stomach.

My body is betraying me.

His eyes linger on mine, and my tongue slides out to lick my lower lip. His eyes darken as he watches my mouth, and the unfamiliar feeling of pure, primal desire floods through me.

The machine beeps.

"Oh! Sorry, Nicole, looks like it was declined. Do you have another card?"

God, I wish she'd keep her voice down. The sexy stranger turns his head toward me as he swipes his card through the turnstile. It clicks open for him, and he steps through. I can feel his eyes on me, and the embarrassment makes my whole head flush red.

"Nicole? Did you want to try another card?"

I nod. "Yeah, here," I say. "Try this one."

The stranger disappears around the corner and I breathe a sigh of relief. I shouldn't be embarrassed—people's cards get declined all the time. But in that specific moment, I wish it hadn't happened to me.

When the second card gets declined, I'm on the edge of tears.

"I'm sorry, Mary," I sigh. "I'm starting a new job tomorrow, so I might just have to forget about a membership for the time being. I can come back in a couple of weeks."

"Hey, no." She sighs, shaking her head. "You're one of our

most dedicated members! Here," she says, swiping my membership card and tapping on the computer. "I've loaded up two weeks for free. Just get your membership paid as soon as you can."

She smiles at me and hands me the card, and I think I might cry. I want to hug her, or run away, or do both. Instead, I just take the card and nod my head.

"Thank you." I want to say more, but my voice chokes up. My heart is still racing from desire and anger and embarrassment.

"Don't mention it." Mary smiles, and then leans toward me. "I mean that. Don't mention it, I'll get in trouble." She grins at me and I laugh, nodding.

"Deal."

This time, when I swipe the card, the turnstile opens and I walk through. It's only a short walk to the women's change room, and I'm able to keep my cool until I close the door.

With a deep, shuddering breath, I wipe my eyes and get changed.

Crying makes me angry now. It feels like I've done nothing but cry over the past year, and I'm completely over it. In the parking lot, it felt good to be mad. It felt good to feel something other than crushing darkness. I let the anger curl in my heart as I think of the stranger. I can still feel the trail of fire that his gaze burned into my skin. It singed my skin and marked me.

... and I liked it.

I walk out toward the pool. It's busy tonight, with half of it cordoned off for lessons. Lap swimmers are contained to two lanes. One of the lanes is marked fast, and it already has three people in it. The other lane only has one man at the far end, so I slide in. The water is cold, and it takes me a second to get used to it. Then, with a deep breath, I start swimming.

When the physical therapist told me that I could start swimming again, it was the only good news I'd gotten in months. Since then, my recovery has been much smoother.

I start swimming freestyle, and the familiar burning in my muscles relaxes me. With every stroke, the stress of the day eases a little bit more. By the time I've reached the other end of the pool, my lungs are starting to work harder, and my body feels like my own again.

At the end of the next lap, the man has caught up to me. He's swimming a lot faster than me, so I wait at the wall and let him turn ahead of me. I frown as he gets closer, and emotion flares in my chest again.

Is that him?

People look different with swim caps and goggles, and he flips at the wall too fast for me to see. His feet kick up and splash me, and then I know. It's him.

I take a deep breath and swim another lap. He catches up to me faster this time, passing me in the middle of the lane. His powerful strokes pull him past me effortlessly, and I'm left dealing with the waves in his wake.

Normally, it wouldn't bother me. But when he passes me a third time, I feel compelled to motion to him at the next wall.

He sputters and stops before turning.

"What?" He asks, lifting his goggles off his eyes. "What do you want?"

"Wow, rude." I move my own goggles to my forehead. "I was just going to say that if you're that fast, you should be in the fast lane. Haven't you ever heard of pool etiquette?"

"I've heard of pool etiquette as much as you've heard of parking lot etiquette."

"And what etiquette is that? That you own the whole thing?"

I'm not usually like this. I don't know what's come over me. Maybe it's his broad, naked chest that's so close to me in the pool. Maybe it's the way the water is dripping down his face and shoulders, or the way he's staring at me with pure anger in his eyes.

Whatever it is, it's making my whole body heat up. Lust flares in the pit of my stomach and I squeeze my thighs together. We're both hanging on to the edge of the wall, facing each other. The man points his thumb at the other lane.

"In case you hadn't noticed, princess, the other lane is full."

"Well then, let's split this one. You stay on your side, and I'll stay on mine. Then we won't have any of these traffic jams. Assuming you're even capable of sharing."

His nostrils flare. His eyes are crushed ice. He stares at me in a way that makes my cheeks flush and my heart skip a beat. My head spins, and I grip the edge of the pool a little bit harder. He's almost incomprehensibly good-looking. He's the kind of sexy that shouldn't even be legal. He's lethal.

"Fine." His jaw tenses as he swallows.

I watch his throat bob up and down and suck my lower lip between my teeth.

"Fine."

He takes a deep breath and pushes off the wall. I watch his back muscles ripple as he pulls himself into the water. My chest heaves as I take a few deep breaths, and then I get on my side of the pool.

4

MARTIN

OF COURSE she would be in my lane. I try not to let it get to me, but as I swim from one end to the other, the heat in my chest starts to grow. Every time we pass each other in the lane —her on her side, me on mine, my anger burns a little hotter.

Finally, I can't take it anymore. For something that was supposed to be relaxing and stress-relieving, it's been the exact opposite. I pull myself out of the pool just as she gets to the wall. She grabs on to the end of it, her chest heaving.

She glances up at me, her eyes travelling from my face down to my chest. I stand, frozen in place by her gaze. She drops her eyes further, and my cock starts to get hard. That filthy tongue of hers swipes across her lower lip. I'd shove my cock straight into her pretty little mouth. That's all she'd be good for.

"You coming back tomorrow?" She asks.

The question surprises me. I shrug. "I usually come every other day."

She nods. "I'll know what days to avoid, then."

A grin twitches at her lips as we stare at each other for a few seconds. Then I nod. "I'll see you around."

"Hopefully not."

I fight the grin off my face. Her smile widens, and she lifts her hand out of the water. Then, she pushes off the wall and is gone.

I grab my towel and dry myself, rubbing my hair as I watch her swim for a few seconds. When I finally walk away, I don't know what to think.

I want to fuck her. No, it's more than that. I want to bury my cock so deep inside her she forgets her own name. I want to wipe that smirk off her face and make her eyes roll back in her head. I want to fill her up with my cum and then have her taste it.

I want to make her mine, if only to show her that I don't appreciate her attitude.

Glancing once more toward the pool, I turn the corner into the change room.

My whole world feels off-balance. I thought the swim would make me forget about Brianne and tire me out. Instead, I feel completely wired. It's like a bolt of lightning has passed through me, in the form of a five-foot four, black-haired, sassy-mouthed vixen.

When I walk out of the change room, I glance toward the pool and feel my pulse speed up. I can still picture the little grin on her face as she waved at me. Blood rushes between my legs. No woman has had this effect on me since...

Well, since Brianne.

My heart hardens again, and I shake my head. A moment of weakness. That's all that was. If I see her again, I'll do her a favor and fuck her like her eyes were begging me to.

Until then, I won't think of her.

I walk out of the building. I avoid the old Honda Civic and walk toward my car, not looking back as I drive away.

. . .

I GET out of bed after another fitful night's sleep. I haven't slept more than four hours a night in the past year. At least I've figured out that a cold shower and two cups of coffee make me feel somewhat normal by the time I get to work.

Somehow, though, I feel more tired than usual today. I make myself a third cup of coffee as I head out the door. By the time I make it to the office, I'm almost starting to feel human again.

But then, the elevator doors open and the sickly-sweet smell of lilies crawls up my nostrils. My mood darkens.

Maybe putting the lilies at the front desk wasn't such a good idea, after all. I should have tossed them in the trash when I had the chance.

I head toward the kitchen, passing Carmen's office along the way. She's a name partner at the firm—Carmen Sanders of the biggest law firm in Denver, Sanders & Perry—and the one who nominated me for my promotion this year. I lean against her doorway.

"Morning, Carmen," I say. She looks up from her computer screen.

"Martin, hi." She takes her glasses off and rubs her eyes. "How long have you been standing there? My head is a wreck. This case is a nightmare."

"The Guildford Media class-action suit?"

She nods. "I'm going to need some extra resources. Would you be able to take it on?"

I think of the ever-growing stack of case files on my desk and then shrug. "Sure. What do you need?"

She points to a box of paperwork. "Those are two of our clients. I need someone to look through the file and start coming up with a strategy. I have a new paralegal starting today, but it'll take a while for her to get up to speed."

"Sure," I say, grabbing the box. "No problem, Boss."

"I'm not your boss anymore."

I grin. "I thought you liked being called boss, Boss."

Carmen just shakes her head, grinning. "Get to work, Henderson. Get me a coffee while you're at it."

"Hey, I'm a partner now, not your assistant. Get your new paralegal to do it."

Carmen just rolls her eyes, dismissing me with a wave.

I lug the heavy box back toward my office. I'm busy, but I've never been one to turn down more work. My mind keeps threatening to go back to the dark-haired tease from the pool yesterday. I need more coffee.

I head to the kitchen and pour two cups of coffee from the pot and head back toward Carmen's office. I may not be her assistant, but I owe her a lot more than a cup of coffee. She looks like her morning has been rougher than mine, if that's even possible.

The door is ajar, so I push it open with my back. When I turn around, I see who Carmen is talking to. That dark hair...

The woman leans over to grab something out of her bag and I almost trip over my own feet. A strangled yelp escapes my lips and the coffee sloshes in one of the cups. I gasp in pain as it spills on my hand, and then I drop the cup on Carmen's white rug.

"Fuck!" I exclaim as the hot coffee burns my palm. Carmen jumps up, and the woman sitting across from her turns around. The woman gets to me before Carmen does, pouring cold water from her water bottle on my hand.

I tense, and then nod, breathing heavily. "Thanks," I say through gritted teeth.

The woman grins at me. It's the same grin she gave me at the pool last night, when I walked away from her.

"You're about as good at delivering coffee as you are at sharing a lane," she says quietly, taking my hand in hers. Her skin is soft and warm, and it sends a jolt of desire rushing toward my cock. Her long, dark eyelashes flutter as she glances at my hand, patting it dry with the sleeve of her shirt.

Carmen comes around her desk and surveys the damage with her hand on her hips. Her rug is ruined, but at least the mug didn't break.

She shakes her head. "You'd be a terrible assistant, Henderson." I pull my hand away from the woman's, but it takes me another second to drag my eyes off her. Carmen nods to the woman. "This is Nicole, my new paralegal. Nicole, this is Martin. He's our best and brightest new partner, if you can believe it." Nicole's eyebrow arches in challenge. My eyes flick to her pink lips.

Carmen continues. "He's the youngest partner the firm has ever had. Don't judge him by his coffee carrying skills."

"Nicole," I say, tasting her name in my mouth.

"I'd shake your hand, but..." she nods to the soaking wet, burning hand. It throbs, and she finishes patting it dry. She drops her hand and I immediately miss her touch.

"I'll get someone over to clean this up," I say, turning on my heels and walking out the doorway. It's not until I get back to my own office that I take a full breath.

She's *here*? She's working for Carmen? In the same office as me?

"Is this a joke?" I say to the ceiling. I imagine Brianne grinning down at me, shrugging. "Is this some twisted joke of yours?"

"Did you say something, boss?" Kelly says as she pokes her head through the door.

I clear my throat, sitting up straighter and shaking my head. "No. Thank you, Kelly. Would you mind getting me another black coffee?"

She nods. "Sure thing."

When she disappears, I slump down in my chair again. My mind is reeling.

I can't work with her!

Nicole.

The name surprises me. It seems too nice for her. She should have a bitchier name.

Nicole.

I scoff and shake my head. What does it matter what her name is? She's here in the same building for the foreseeable future. Working alongside one of the firm's name partners. Working alongside *me.*

And all I can think about is how much I'd like to shove my cock in every single hole of hers.

Great.

5

NICOLE

CARMEN'S ASSISTANT shows me to my desk. I look around the massive office, trying to see where Martin's office is. I wasn't expecting his name to be Martin. I don't know what I was expecting, but it wasn't that.

My heart is still racing. I wish I hadn't been so rude at the pool; he's basically my boss now.

I sit down at my desk and righteous anger starts building up in the pit of my stomach.

No. I don't regret being rude at the pool. *He* was the rude one! Who cares if he's my coworker? I'm working for Carmen. I can be civil to him, and I'll just stay out of his way. If anything, it's a good thing I stood my ground at the pool! Guys like him are just bullies. They need boundaries.

Still, the way his eyes travelled up my body when he saw me made my heart skip a beat. What boundary is that? I'd set boundaries just to hope he tore them down.

Yes, I definitely need to stay out of his way.

I need to stay far, far away from those ocean-blue eyes. From those broad, strong hands. I close my eyes and all I can see is him standing next to the pool, with water dripping down every ridge and valley of muscle on his perfectly chiseled body.

Fuck.

I'm in trouble.

I jump when someone says my name.

"I'm Neil, from IT," a tall young man says. His shirt is untucked and his tie is crooked. He nods to a laptop in his hands. "You want to get this set up?"

I force a smile. "Sure."

His eyes are kind. They're soft blue, and they have nowhere near the intensity of Martin's gaze. He slides a chair over to my desk and opens the laptop. I take a deep breath to calm my frazzled nerves and inhale the scent of cheap aftershave. Neil smells like a teenager on a first date.

He smiles at me, nodding to the screen. "Just choose a password and we can get started."

IT TAKES a couple hours to get paperwork sorted out and to do a couple training sessions. I meet about a thousand people and I remember almost no one's name. When I'm back at my desk, I sit down and try to catch my breath. First days are always overwhelming.

Then, Martin appears around the corner and 'overwhelming' becomes the understatement of the century. He's carrying a thick file under his arm. His long, purposeful strides ooze power. His eyes find mine, and my insides turn to warm goo.

My heartbeat speeds up when I realize he's heading straight toward me.

"Carmen says she's assigned you to the Guildford case." He drops the file on my desk without preamble.

"Oh?" I smooth my hands over my pencil skirt. "Okay."

He motions to the file. "Look through this paperwork. We're expecting Guildford to submit a motion to dismiss, and we're going to need to counter it. I need you to organize it as per the notes that I've made on the front page. We need the evidence grouped by type. I'll need three copies of the file once it's organized."

I nod. I guess Sanders & Perry is a 'sink or swim' kind of firm. I pull the file closer to me and Martin starts to walk away.

"How's your hand?"

He pauses, glancing over his shoulder at me. "It's fine. I need that by eight o'clock this evening."

I watch him walk away as anger starts to boil inside me. There's no need to be so rude! I was just asking how his potential second-degree burn was doing. Fuck me, right?

But I guess he's the all-important rising star partner at the firm, and I'm just a lowly paralegal. That explains his attitude at the pool. He probably thinks he's God's gift to the world. Of course he would think he owns the parking spaces and the pool lanes. He thinks he owns the whole fucking city.

And now I have to work with him. Lucky-fucking-me.

I fume as I open up the file and start reading it. I haven't done any paralegal work in almost eighteen months, and my nerves have been strained all week. When I start reading the file though, the familiarity of the work makes my shoulders relax. I can do this, and I can deal with stupid, arrogant, sexy-as-sin Martin Henderson like a professional.

"He's not as bad as he seems," a voice says behind me. I turn to see a young woman about my age. She nods down the hallway. "Martin."

"He seems pretty bad."

She grins. "Try working for him."

"Are you a junior lawyer?"

That makes her laugh. She shakes her head. "I'm his assistant. I'm the Donna to his Harvey," she grins. "Minus the sexual tension."

"I've only seen a couple episodes of Suits," I say. "But Harvey seemed like an asshole."

The woman extends her hand, grinning. "Kelly."

"Nicole."

"Here," she says, putting a mug of coffee on my desk. "I don't apologize for Martin often but call it a peace offering."

"You should never apologize for anyone." I take the coffee with a smile. "He's a big boy, and if he wants to apologize, he can do it himself."

She nods, chewing her lip. "If I tell you something, will you promise not to tell him I said it?" I nod, making a mental note not to share any of my own secrets with her. Does she even remember my name?

Kelly takes a deep breath. "Yesterday was the one-year anniversary of his wife's death. She was pregnant."

My eyebrows shoot up.

Oh.

Of all people, I know how he feels. I nod at Kelly.

"I see."

"Don't judge him based on this week."

"That seems fair. Thanks for the coffee."

"Anytime," she says. "Let me know if you want to grab lunch sometime." Her smile is genuine, and I feel myself relax ever so slightly. Maybe this place won't be so bad, after all. As long as Mr. Big Shot stays out of my way.

That's unkind of me.

I take a deep breath and close my eyes. Last Thursday was the one-year anniversary of Jack's death, and I was a mess. I didn't leave my bed the whole day. If Martin's day yesterday was anything like mine last Thursday, he was going through hell.

Except he went to work all day and then he had to deal with me being snarky and rude to him at the pool. He was probably just there for the same reason I was—to let off some steam and try to forget about how shitty life is.

I sigh as embarrassment floods through me. I glance up toward Martin's office and chew my lip. Should I say something?

Then I remember his attitude when he walked away from me, and a wave of righteous anger floods through me. Even though he was going through something tough, it doesn't mean he has to take it out on *me*! We're all going through tough shit! Having a hard week doesn't excuse being an arrogant ass about it.

Complicated emotions battle in my heart. I want to be empathetic, but whenever I think of the scowl on Martin's face, it just makes something else spark inside me. Anger and desire battle with compassion. The thought of him makes the fire inside me burn hotter than it has in months.

So, instead of trying to figure out what's going on inside me, I turn to the file and start working.

For a moment, I stare at the pages and take a deep breath. If this is my first day and things have started so dramatically, maybe I should look for something else. All I want is a quiet job to pull in a decent paycheck. I just want to start paying off some of my debts until Jack's life insurance money comes through.

The last thing I need is drama. I don't think my heart can take it.

6

MARTIN

It's just past 7 p.m. when Nicole comes into my office. She has a big box in her arms and lifts it up slightly, questioning me with a look.

"Put it down on the table there," I say, gesturing to the coffee table that had Brianne's lilies on it yesterday. Nicole drops the box down and pulls out one thick folder.

"As requested, I organized the evidence chronologically and by client. Here." She hands me a folder.

I'm impressed. When I said I needed it by 8 p.m., I was exaggerating by about twenty-four hours. I didn't think she'd actually finish it today. I push myself back from my desk and walk over to her. I take the folder she hands me and flick through it, nodding.

"Good."

She shifts from foot to foot. "Looks like an interesting case. Guildford Media is huge. I had no idea they had so many complaints from employees."

"Our clients tell us that they've been keeping salaries capped and systematically preventing anyone from moving up the ladder."

"Especially women." She tilts her head to the side and glances at me. Her eyes are dark grey, with little flecks of brown in them. My gaze drops down to her lips and her tongue slides out to lick them. Something stirs in the pit of my stomach, and I clear my throat.

"It certainly appears to be the case," I say. I pull a couple more folders out of the box and bring them to my desk. It's not until I sit down that I realize Nicole is still there. She's staring at me, and then nods and turns toward the door.

I watch her pause as she sees something on the floor next to the couch. She bends over, and I can't help but notice the way her skirt stretches over her perfect, round ass.

Shaking my head, I look down at the files. This is bad. Work is work, and sex is sex. The two do not meet in my world, ever. I went through six assistants before finding Kelly. They all figured when they threw themselves at me, I'd let them suck my cock and not expect them to do their job. Kelly's the first one who hasn't had any interest in anything more than a professional relationship.

But now...

I can't resist looking up when Nicole stands up. She holds up a lily bloom.

"It was next to the couch." She shakes her head. "This place must have a thing for lilies. The smell is nauseating when you walk out of the elevators. I nearly quit on the spot when I walked in."

I arch my eyebrow. She grins, bringing the flower to my desk. She places it gently next to my computer monitor. A ring glints on her finger, and disappointment fills my chest.

Of course she's married.

Poor fucker. I bet she's a nightmare.

Her fingers linger on the edge of my desk. "I was wondering what the stench in here was. I was worried it was you." Her eyes sparkle as a grin twitches at the corners of her lips.

I pick up the flower. My fingers brush hers and a current of warmth runs up my arm. Her eyes linger on mine as I look at the flower, and a blush creeps over her cheeks

"I hate lilies too." I finger the bloom, feeling its velvety soft petals between my fingers. My eyes flick to Nicole's pink lips.

"Yeah?"

I nod. "My mom sent me these yesterday. I almost threw them out, but then I decided to bring them to the front desk."

Her mouth drops open and she nods, as if she understands everything. "I see."

Does she see? Does she know about Brianne? How could she know?

"It's a clever tactic." She tilts her head to the side and grins. "Disarm people right when they walk out the elevator. They can't think about settlements or negotiations when they're worried about breathing through their nose."

I chuckle, placing the lily back down on my desk. I'd throw it out, but it feels wrong.

I nod to the box on the table. "Good work today. I didn't think you'd be able to do it."

Nicole rolls her eyes. "Oh wow, another man who underestimates my abilities and intellect. What else is new?" She shakes her head and walks toward the door. Her hand drifts up the door frame as she turns her head.

"I'm going to the pool tonight."

My eyebrows lift up. "Okay..." *Is that an invitation*?

"I'll take Tuesday, Thursday, and Saturday if you want Monday, Wednesday, and Friday."

Ah.

I nod. "Sure." Why is it that I'm tongue tied when she's

around? Maybe it's because my tongue is too busy wondering what she tastes like. I watch her hips sway from side to side as she walks out the door and around the corner, and I let out a sigh.

For the first time since Brianne died, a current of energy makes me sit up straighter. My hands tremble as I open the folders in front of me, and I frown to keep my vision focused.

Every time I hear heels clicking on the floor outside my office, my ears perk up. Every time it's a woman other than Nicole that walks by, disappointment creeps into my chest. I hate myself for it. I hate how weak I feel, how out of control I am today.

Forty-five minutes later, Nicole walks by my door. She doesn't look toward me.

I take a deep breath and weave my fingers together behind my head. I lean back in my chair and stare at the ceiling, blowing the air out of my mouth.

This is pathetic. I don't even like her! She's rude, snarky, and makes me feel like I'm a total asshole most of the time.

I mean, I *am* an asshole most of the time, but when I'm around her I don't enjoy it quite so much as usual.

I stand up, slamming the folders closed. I rush to the elevator and head toward the underground parking lot. Jogging past my own car, I scan the parking lot for the beat-up Honda Civic. She's just pulling out of her space, and I jog toward the end of the parking lot. Waving my arms, I run toward her car. My tie flips up over my shoulder and my black dress shoes slap on the cold concrete. She comes to a stop in front of me, frowning.

My breath comes out in puffs in front of my face, but I don't feel cold. There's too much fire in my veins for that.

She rolls her window down—yes, literally rolls it down—and sticks her head out the window.

"What's wrong?"

"I can't do this."

She stares at me like I have three heads. I comb my fingers through my hair—maybe to make sure that I, in fact, only have one head.

"You can't do Monday-Wednesday-Friday?"

"No! I mean *this*," I point between her and me. "Banter and joking around. This is work, Nicole." *And you're married.*

"I understand that," she bristles. Her eyes narrow and she shakes her head. "You're the one who came out here and ran after *me*, remember? I've done exactly what you've asked, and more. It's my first day and I know the Guildford Media case almost as well as you do. If that's not work what the fuck do you call it?"

"I know. I just... Fuck, I don't know." My head is so fucked up. When I look at her, I see Brianne. Well, I don't *see* Brianne, but I see a seed of her inside Nicole. They're both headstrong and stubborn and able to stand up to me.

Nicole shakes her head and taps on her horn three times.

"Alright. Out of the way, Big Shot," she snips.

She rolls the car forward until she's level with me. She stares at me for a few moments and shakes her head. Her eyes are blazing, and the laughter is gone from them.

"I'm just here to collect a paycheck, nothing more." She swallows. "If you don't like me, I can stay out of your way. Maybe you can talk to Carmen about taking me off the Guildford Media case."

I nod. A lump forms in my throat. *It's not that I don't like you,* I want to tell her. *It's that I* do *like you.*

A smile twitches at her lips and she shakes her head. "You know, the minute you jumped out of your car in the pool parking lot, I knew you were crazy."

"Who are you calling crazy?"

"Oh, gee, I don't know. Maybe the man that ran after me to remind me that I'm here to do a job? The guy who's standing in this freezing cold parking garage telling me that I need to focus? The guy who doesn't know basic parking lot etiquette?"

"*I* don't know basic parking lot etiquette? Me? Are you fucking kidding me?"

She rolls her eyes, shaking her head. When she looks at me again, her eyebrow arches.

"Are you serious?"

"Deadly."

She laughs humorlessly and gives me a little wave. "Don't worry, Big Shot. I won't bother you anymore, as long as you stop following me around."

My jaw drops open, but before I can respond she drives away.

Idiot! What did that accomplish? All I did was make myself look like a total lunatic.

Maybe she's right. I'll talk to Carmen in the morning and get her to give the Guildford Media stuff to one of the other paralegals. I'll make up some excuse.

I know one thing—I can't be in the same room as Nicole under any circumstances.

7

NICOLE

I RAGE-SWIM until my body is exhausted. With every kick, every stroke, every breath, I just think about Martin's stupid sexy scowl. Who is *he* to tell me that I need to take work seriously? Did he not see the amazing work I dropped on his desk this evening?

Is this because I said lilies were dumb, stinky flowers? Maybe they suit his dumb, stinky face.

I flip at the wall and kick off, gliding under water until my muscles burn and my lungs are screaming. I come up and swim faster than I've swam since before the accident. By the time my workout is over, my chest is heaving and my whole body feels tired. My back aches, and the pain runs down my side in deep throbs.

I take a deep, painful breath. I went too hard.

I'll blame Martin for that, too.

Pulling myself out of the water, I sit on the edge of the pool and catch my breath. I run my hands along my side, waiting for the familiar pulsing pain to stop.

It eases more quickly than usual. I take a deep breath, filling up my lungs down to the very bottom. Usually, that would make my ribs ache down to the marrow, but this time it doesn't. I take another deep breath, but pain doesn't come back.

Maybe I'm actually getting better.

Maybe the pain that's plagued me for a year is finally starting to ease off. It's that agonizing physical reminder of everything that I've lost—the pain that continually reminds me that I, unfortunately, survived.

I stare at the clock on the wall, spinning around and around as swimmers time their laps. Time marches on, and it doesn't matter whether I'm in pain or not. Time doesn't care about my pain, my body, or my grief. I stare at the clock until my skin prickles into goosebumps and I realize I'm cold.

Pulling my goggles and swim cap off my head, I pad toward the change rooms. I glance toward the entrance, almost hoping to see Martin waiting for me.

I shake my head.

Why would I think that? Why would one of the partners at Sanders & Perry, Denver's most prestigious law firm, be waiting for me to finish swimming? I snort at myself and head for the showers. It's not until the hot water hits my cold skin that I start feeling like myself again. I stretch my body from side to side, feeling for any aches or niggles that might be hiding in the corners of my body.

I smile when I can move with only a bit of aching in my side.

At least Martin was good for one thing. I haven't pushed myself that hard in swimming for fear of hurting myself. It just took a bit of good old-fashioned anger and outrage to make me realize that my barriers were mental, not physical.

When I pull dry clothes onto my freshly washed body, I breathe a sigh of contentment.

"I hope you'd be proud of me," I say under my breath as I

reach for my wedding ring. I take it out of my bag and look at it for a few moments. Tiredness settles into my spirit as I remember all that I've lost.

Jack used to tell me that if anything happened to him, he wanted me to move on as quickly as possible. Easier said than done, Jack. I slip the ring onto my finger, just as I've done every day since the day we were married. Except this time, I hesitate.

I unclasp the gold chain around my neck and slip my ring onto it. When I tie it back around my neck, I touch the cool metal against my breastbone and take a deep breath. I glance at my finger—so naked now, without the rings that I've worn for years.

When I stand up, I almost expect the rings to weigh me down like a yoke around my neck. Instead, I feel lighter. I touch the ring once more and then sling my bag over my shoulder.

MARTIN SEEMS to calm down over the course of the week. Another paralegal comes on the case, and he mostly communicates with her. Carmen gives me work from two more cases to do, and Martin and I learn to coexist.

As much as I hate myself for it, it still gives me a little thrill every time he walks by.

On Friday, I walk into the kitchen to see him standing by the coffee machine. He's not wearing a tie and the top button of his shirt is undone. My eyes linger on the little triangle of skin a bit longer than they should. Heat zips through my spine and I glance at his eyes.

He's watching me. Sometimes it feels like he's always watching me. We hardly speak to each other, but I know that he senses when I walk in. Every time we're in the same room, his spine stiffens, and he meets my gaze for a brief moment.

"Careful with that thing," I say, nodding to the machine.

His eyes stare at mine for a few moments, and then drop to my lips. I watch him glance at my body, my breasts, my legs, and then turn back to the coffee machine. All the blood rushes to my center, and I think I might pass out.

"It's a hazard," he finally says, pouring himself a mug. "You want some?"

"You sure you can handle it?"

His lips twitch. What would he look like if he smiled—I mean really smiled?

He glances at me for the briefest moment and then nods. When he hands me the coffee cup, my fingers brush his and my heart palpitates. I nod in thanks.

"Good work on the Guildford Media case," he says, leaning against the counter. He drags his hand through his hair, mussing it slightly. I resist the urge to fix it, instead gripping my mug a little tighter.

"Thanks. You guys think you'll get a settlement?"

"They've made an acceptable offer. We just have to get our clients to agree to it."

"Easier said than done," I laugh. "I remember another class-action that I worked on about six years ago. It was a dream settlement, and it all fell through because of one man. Ed Drury—I'll never forget him."

His eyes have settled on my hands, and he frowns. "You're not wearing your wedding ring."

My eyebrows shoot up, and I glance at my hand. "Is that a problem?"

"No, I just... Are you...? Is everything okay?" He scratches his ear and clears his throat.

I laugh. "Are you a marriage counselor now?"

"Forget it."

"If I didn't know what a jerk you were, I would think that you cared."

He turns away from me, and I laugh again. I pull the chain around my neck out from underneath my shirt. I show him the rings and smile.

"My husband died last year." My voice sounds small, but it feels good to say it out loud. His eyes widen and his lips drop open in a small 'o'.

"Car accident. Hit and run."

"I'm sorry."

"Me too," I say, snorting bitterly. There's a silence between us. I don't want to tell him I know about his wife, but I feel like we share something that no one else understands. He stares in my eyes and sees my pain. I know he does, because I see the grief swimming in his eyes. Maybe that's why we get under each other's skin so much.

"My wife died last year as well." He takes a sip of coffee and then stares at the liquid in his mug. "She was at risk of miscarrying and had to have an emergency C-section." He swallows, and his Adam's apple bobs up and down. "She never woke up from it. Died a couple days later."

"Oh." I take a step closer to him. "And the baby?"

He shakes his head, and then inhales sharply. His lips purse and his eyes go cloudy. When he finally turns to me, my heart cracks under the weight of our shared pain. Martin gives me a sad smile.

"Maybe that's why you bother me so much, Nicole."

God, it sounds good when he says my name. I want to put my hand on his arm and feel the warmth of his body. I want to stroke his cheek and rub his head until he groans in satisfaction, but I just stand there, painfully close and painfully far.

I clear my throat. "I bother you?"

"Horribly."

"Well at least we have that in common."

"You don't have the nauseating positivity of people who haven't lost. I can't hate you like I can hate everyone else."

That makes me laugh. I shrug. "I never knew being bitter, jaded, and alone was such a great personality trait."

"Neither did I." His grin widens, and my heart explodes in my chest. It's almost a real smile, and it's blinding. He has dimples—two of them. His perfect teeth could be in a Colgate commercial, if they needed ultra-sexy lawyers to represent their toothpaste.

Then, his smile fades and the moment's over. He drains his mug. "I'll need copies of the settlement offer for this afternoon's meeting."

I nod. "Yes, sir."

Martin's eyes flash as he glances at me. Then, he walks out of the kitchen and I'm alone.

8

MARTIN

THE GUILDFORD MEDIA case gets settled out of court, and Carmen assigns Nicole to other cases that have nothing to do with me.

When that case ends, so does most of our interaction. I shouldn't care, but I do. She doesn't slip into my office to give me some files anymore or lean against my desk as she chews on the end of her pen. She doesn't give me shit for being an arrogant ass.

A week after the case finishes, I walk in on her near the copy machine, laughing at something that the IT guy says. His hand drifts to her shoulder and she wraps hers around his back in a half-hug. Anger bursts through my chest. He must sense my gaze, because the IT guy drops his hand. Nicole turns to follow his gaze and frowns at me.

I march away from them, cursing myself.

Why the fuck would I care if she wants to fuck what's-his-name from IT?

I get back to my office and slam the door behind me, but someone stops it from closing. Nicole stands in the doorway, her long dark hair falling in soft waves around her face. She's wearing red lipstick today, and I wish those perfect lips were getting messy all over my cock.

"What do you want?"

"What the fuck is your problem? You scared Neil half to death! He thinks you're going to fire him."

"I should."

"For what?"

"For touching you inappropriately."

"Excuse me?"

"He had his hands all over you."

My heart is racing. She takes a step inside and shuts the door with her foot. I stand my ground as she walks toward me until we're chest to chest.

"What is wrong with you, Martin?" She's asking it as if it's a serious question. As if she wants to know what, in fact, is wrong with me.

"He shouldn't be touching you."

"He wasn't."

"He had his hand on your shoulder."

"What, like this?" She puts her hand on my shoulder and my breath hitches. "Are you going to fire me now?"

"Stop it."

"No, you stop it. You're a moody fucker, you know that, Martin? Maybe if your head wasn't stuck so far up your ass, you'd actually be able to form meaningful relationships with people instead of skulking like some bratty teenager."

Her hand squeezes my shoulder. It drifts down slightly, and I know she can feel my heartbeat. Her grey eyes look almost silver in this light, and her cheeks are bright red. My hands are itching to brush along her jaw and cup her face, but instead I just turn away.

"You should leave now."

"Why?"

"Because I don't want you here! I have work to do."

"Martin." She takes a step toward me, and I feel her hand on my arm.

I glance at her, shaking my head. "Just go."

"Neil just lost his dog. He's a mess right now, and he doesn't need you scaring him half to death."

"That's just a lame excuse to put his hands all over you. I know what men are like, Nicole."

Her eyebrows arch and a grin plays over her lips. "Why, Mr. Henderson, if I didn't know any better, I'd think you were jealous!"

"I've got work to do."

Her hand lingers on my arm until I sigh.

"I'll apologize to Neil. I'll go easy on him."

A smile spreads on her lips and she nods. "Good."

I watch her walk out the door and let out a frustrated sigh. The thought of another man touching Nicole makes my blood boil. She ignites every possessive, animalistic, jealous bone in my body. She makes my blood run hotter and my entire body feel like it's on high alert.

She makes me feel alive.

So, three weeks later, when a pro bono case gets dropped on my desk, my heart goes to my throat. I have to take the case, for Brianne and for myself, but it'll be the hardest case of my career. I can only see one way of me taking on this case without going crazy. I go to Carmen's office and ask for Nicole to work on it with me.

Carmen's eyebrow arches.

"You want me to take my most efficient paralegal off

paying cases, and put her on this pro bono case? You do realize that we're in the business of making money, right?"

"Everyone else is snowed under," I say. It's true, but that wouldn't normally stop me from asking them to do more work. This time, though, it's different. I need Nicole.

Carmen sighs, tenting her fingers in front of her chest as she leans back in her chair. She sighs.

"Fine. But if this interferes with any of her other work, I'm taking her off it."

I fight to keep the smile off my face. Instead, I just nod. "Understood."

When I head back to Nicole's desk, my heart is thumping. I haven't spoken to her in a couple days, and it's like I'm fiending for her. I need a hit of my favorite drug. I need that sweet, floral perfume-wearing, peach-assed, sassy-mouthed drug.

When she's not at her desk, I frown. I turn to Clarissa, another paralegal.

"Any idea where Nicole is?"

"She left at lunch, said she had a doctor's appointment."

"Is she coming back?"

Clarissa shrugs at me. "Do you want her phone number? You can call her and ask."

I sigh, running my hands through my hair. I wasn't expecting this. I'd wanted to brief her on the case and get started right away. I nod to Clarissa.

"Sure."

She gives me the number, and I take it back to my office, closing the door behind me. Why am I nervous right now? I'm calling a coworker about a work-related matter. Nothing to be nervous about.

Still, my palms feel clammy and my mouth has gone dry. I take a sip of water and then sigh in frustration.

"Nicole," I say when she answers. "How are you?"

"I'm okay," she says. "What's up?"

"Carmen's just given me a pro bono case and wants you on it with me." *A little white lie never hurt anyone.*

"Okay," she answers. I hear her shuffling something and then she makes a noise. "I should be done here in an hour, and I can come to your office as soon as I'm back. I'm at the doctor."

"No problem."

The hour crawls by. Finally, a light rap on the door tells me that Nicole is here.

"Hey, Big Shot," she says, poking her head through.

"Stop calling me that."

"Isn't that what you are?" She says, closing the door behind her. The room gets a couple degrees warmer.

Nicole takes a step toward the bookcases lining the wall, running her long, slender fingers along the spines of leather-bound books.

"You've got your fancy law books, your fancy degrees, your fancy car. Youngest partner in the firm's history." She glances at me, grinning. "If that isn't a big shot, I don't know what is."

I grin. "Fine. I'm a big deal."

She laughs and comes to sit down across the desk from me. We stare at each other for a few moments until she spreads her palms.

"You rang?"

I nod. "New case. Pro bono."

"I didn't know big shot lawyers took cases for free."

I grin. "I don't, usually. This one matters."

I slide the file to her and watch as she flicks it open. Her eyebrows shoot up. "Medical misconduct in relation to an expecting mother. She lost the baby. Isn't this a bit close to home?"

"That's why I can't turn it down. And you're the only one who will understand that."

She glances at the papers again and nods solemnly. "I do."

"Good."

I launch into a brief of the case as Nicole takes notes. She sits up straight, listening closely. I watch her pen move across the page as she writes, and my eyes drift up to her chest. Her shirt dips down to show her collarbone and I imagine what it would feel like to run my fingers across it—or my tongue. I stumble over my words, and Nicole looks up.

"Sorry," I say.

"S'okay," she says, sticking the end of her pen into her mouth. "So what's your defense strategy?"

"Establish a pattern of behavior. Discredit witnesses. The usual."

She nods. A strand of hair falls from her bun to the side of her face, and all I want to do is tuck it back behind her ear. Instead, I clear my throat and stand up.

"I'll help you with these boxes," I say. "You can get started with these two."

"Sure."

I come around the desk and stand next to her as I grab one of the file boxes. She leans over at the same time, and I catch a whiff of her perfume. She smells womanly, sweet, delicate. My cock throbs against my leg as her scent envelops me. I clear my throat and pick up the box, taking a step away from her.

My head is spinning. Nicole opens the door and holds it with her leg as I walk through. Neither of us speaks until we're at her desk. Her eyes flick to me, and she nods.

"I'll get you the first motion drafted by this evening."

"Good." I clear my throat, and then drum my knuckles on her desk. I inhale, and then nod. Turning back toward the hallway, I walk with as much purpose as I can muster. I can feel her eyes on my back, and I force myself not to turn around to check.

9

NICOLE

"WHAT'S GOING ON THERE?" Clarissa says, leaning toward me. She pokes her head above the cubicle partition to see Martin walking away.

"What do you mean?"

She looks at me with an arched eyebrow.

"I've never seen Martin Henderson help anyone with boxes of files, ever. Even when he was a junior lawyer."

I frown. "What? Really?"

Clarissa nods. "Either he likes you, or he's worried about something else. I know which one I think it is," she grins.

"It's probably just the case," I reply. My heart thumps and I glance down the hallway after him. What if it isn't just the case? I shake my head and take a deep breath. He told me when I first started that this is work, and work needs to be respected. I agree with that. We haven't crossed any lines.

Besides, he's so hot and cold that I can't keep up. He definitely doesn't seem to *like* me. In any case, we've been able to work together for nearly two months, so why would this be any different?

. . .

It is different, though. I learn that over the next two weeks. Martin and I work more closely together than we have before, and I realize why he was made partner. Even with the rest of his paying caseload, he puts his heart and soul into the pro bono case.

On Thursday night, the two of us stay late to finish up some work that needs to be submitted to the court Friday morning. I'm sitting on the sofa in his office, and I glance up at him. His fingers are threaded through his hair as he leans over the files. He's writing furiously, and the light of his desk lamp is illuminating all the angles of his face.

He's terribly handsome. He's terribly handsome and terribly, heartbreakingly unavailable.

Then again—what am I? I'm the definition of unavailable.

Sensing me looking at him, he glances up. His tongue slides out to lick his lips, and then he stretches his arms up over his head and cracks his neck.

"How do you feel about Chinese food?"

"I feel pretty good about Chinese food."

He picks up his phone. "I'm getting some. My stomach is rumbling."

"I think my stomach has developed an entire language in the past thirty minutes." I drop a file back on the coffee table and lean back on the sofa. "It hasn't stopped making noise. I'm surprised you haven't heard it from over there."

Martin grins. "I didn't want to say anything, but..."

"Why, Mr. Henderson! Did you just make a joke?"

I put my hand to my chest and drop my jaw in mock surprise. He grins wide enough for his dimples to appear, and then balls up a piece of paper and throws it at me. It falls to the floor a couple feet short and I shake my head.

"Good thing you went into law and not basketball."

"Watch your mouth, Martinez. I could have you fired."

I snort, arching an eyebrow. "Is that supposed to impress me?"

"It's supposed to scare you."

"Try harder."

His eyes blaze through me, leaving me breathless from across the room. My panties are suddenly soaked, as they so often are when Martin turns his eyes on me. I shift in my seat and turn back to my work.

I smell the food before I see it. My ears perk up at the sound of footsteps in the hallway. When the delivery driver gives us the food, it takes all my self-control not to descend on it like a wild dog.

Martin hands me a container and I tuck in. He comes to sit next to me on the couch, and we both groan in contentment.

"Good call."

"Sometimes being a big shot is a good thing." He sticks his chopsticks into a container of noodles.

I laugh. We both lean back on the couch and eat in silence. Finally, I turn to him.

"What happened with your wife? You think it was medical misconduct?"

He sighs, shaking his head. "I don't know. It's a blur. I don't really remember that week at all. Doctors were constantly asking me to make decisions and to sign things and consent to this procedure and that procedure. We lost the baby right away, and I think I was just in shock."

I nod, poking at my food.

"She was fine," he says. "She was fine, and then the next thing I know, she's in the hospital. I wasn't even there when she passed out—I was at work." His voice tightens, and the muscles in his jaw twitch. He sighs, shaking his head. "I guess with this case, I feel like at least I can make a difference in one person's life. It won't bring Brianne back, but she'd have liked me taking the case."

We eat in silence for a few minutes.

"I think the shock makes it worse," I hear myself saying. "Jack and I were up in Aspen skiing for the weekend. We were driving back on Sunday evening and then got side swiped by a car. We spun into a tree. Jack died, and I broke my back."

"You broke your back?"

I grimace. "Yeah. I had to learn to walk again, and I only got cleared for work a couple months ago after begging my doctor to clear me. Thank fuck, because the medical bills were starting to become a problem."

"Did Jack not have life insurance?"

I snort bitterly.

Martin shakes his head. "Sorry. I don't mean to pry."

"No, we did. That's what makes this whole thing so messed up. The insurance company keeps stalling. They've asked me for Jack's medical records about four times so far, and they keep asking me about the ski trip. It's like they're gearing up to deny the claim. I think they might try to say that skiing isn't covered in the policy, even though we were driving. I'm getting to the point where I don't really care. Why would I care about money when everything else has gone to shit?"

"Fucking insurance companies," Martin spits. "They just prey on vulnerable people."

I chuckle and take another bite of noodles. "I don't know why I'm telling you this stuff. I didn't mean to hijack the conversation. We were talking about you."

"It's all the same," Martin says, putting his hand on my knee. The touch sends my head spinning. My heart bounces off my ribcage and I glance at him. Without realizing what I'm doing, I put my hand over his.

"Life just sucks sometimes." His hand tightens on my knee, sending another flutter of heartbeats through my chest.

"It does."

"Sometimes I feel like I'm just trying to make it suck a little bit less."

I tighten my fingers around his and smile. His eyes drop to my lips, and heat burns through my body. I squeeze my thighs together. My breath is shallow, and I don't want to move.

Then, Martin pulls his hand away. I straighten up, biting back my disappointment.

What did I expect? That he would ravage me right here in his office?

I clear my throat, stacking the takeout containers and wiping my lips on a napkin.

"Thanks for the food... And the chat."

"Let's get this done and get out of here," he says. "I know it's time to call it a night when I'm rambling about my status as a widower."

"You weren't rambling." I put the takeout containers in a neat stack on the table and then turn to him. His eyes linger on mine, and then he nods.

"You're not as bad as I thought you were that day at the pool."

I burst out laughing. "Gee, thanks. You sure know how to make a girl feel special."

A grin spreads across his lips and he shrugs. "Just being honest."

"Well, if we're being honest, you're not as insufferable as I thought you were either."

"Insufferable! That's rich, coming from you." He shifts on the couch and his thigh brushes against mine. I bite my lip.

"I think you like me talking back to you. You like the fact that I don't put up with your shit."

"I wouldn't go that far. But the fact that you're strong-willed does have a certain... appeal." His voice is a low growl. It sends primal desire tingling through my body, from my fingertips to my toes. My whole body screams at me to touch him, grab him, kiss him, never let him go.

I sit, unmoving.

My breath catches in my throat. His thigh is still touching mine, and it feels like all the blood in my body is rushing between my legs. I swallow.

I can't think straight. The heat coming from his body is making my head spin. Why does he have to smell so freaking good all the time? His eyes are staring into mine and I could get lost in them. His chest rises and falls with every breath, and I inhale. The fresh, manly scent of his cologne fills my nostrils and another wave of desire washes over me.

He leans closer to me, sliding his arm across the back of the couch. My heart hammers. My eyes flick to his lips, and my tongue slides out to lick my own. He follows the movement, moving his other hand to my thigh. It slides up the inside of my leg as he moves closer. I lean into him and—

His phone rings.

He freezes, dropping his chin to his chest. He pulls the phone out of his pocket and clears his throat, glancing at me.

I shift away from him, picking up the empty takeout containers. I stand up as he answers the phone, busying myself with tidying up. He stands up and I walk out of the office to get rid of the containers. By the time I come back, he's sitting behind his desk.

He keeps his head down as I walk in. "If you make copies of the exhibits, I'll be able to put this together now. You can get out of here, then. Get some rest."

"Sure," I say, gathering the documents. I steal a glance toward him, but I already know the moment is gone.

10

MARTIN

NICOLE and I wave awkwardly to each other in the parking lot and go our separate ways. I take my time getting in my car, giving her enough time to drive away.

With a deep sigh, I put my hands on the steering wheel and lean my forehead against it. That was too far. I almost kissed her. Fuck knows I *wanted* to kiss her.

I don't know whether to be relieved or disappointed that I didn't. I take a deep breath and sit back in my seat.

Then, I put my car in gear and drive out after her. Instead of turning toward home, I head in the opposite direction. I can't be alone right now, I need to take the edge off.

I park the car outside the bar. 'Jaime's Bar' shines back at me in bright lights—he's had the sign redone. The front of the building has also been repainted, and the place isn't looking half bad. The last time I visited my best friend—when was it, exactly? Six months ago? —his bar was looking run down. I get out and lock my car, heading for the entrance.

As soon as I walk in, I hear my name being called. Jaime's behind the bar, arms extended toward me.

"Marty!" A smile spreads across his face. "Buddy!"

I grin and my shoulders relax a bit. I slide onto a stool at the end of the bar. Jaime shakes my hand, and then leans on the bar between us.

"To what do I owe the honor?" He grins. "You haven't been out on a school night since our undergrad years."

"And you haven't been *in* on a school night since then."

Jaime laughs, grabs a rag and starts wiping the bar down. "That's the life of a bar owner."

"Sometimes I think you were the smart one."

"You think?" His eyes twinkle as he grins. They're still as bright blue as when we were in college, even if his hairline has receded a few inches. I'm sure I don't look like the bright-eyed, bushy-tailed young man I was then, either.

I grin. "Yeah. I thought you were crazy for dropping out and buying this place, but now look. You're happier and healthier than I am."

"You work too much, man."

"Yeah. I have no choice, man. I'm like a shark—if I stop swimming, I die."

"Is that true, about sharks? I always thought that was a myth."

I shrug. "I don't know, I'm not a biologist."

Jaime grins, shaking his head. "I thought you were gone forever. Haven't seen you much since..." He trails off.

"Since Brianne died."

His eyebrows arch. "Yeah. Since Brianne died. I've also never heard you say those words out loud."

"No?" I clear my throat. Jaime reaches up to the top shelf and pulls down a bottle. Then, he pours me a big drink and slides it toward me. I nod. "I've thought about it a lot. I figured I would have mentioned it once or twice."

"Grief is a funny thing."

I take a deep breath and stare at the glass. It's his finest scotch, a bottle I bought him for his wedding. He usually only lets me or his wife drink it.

One of the other bar patrons yells across the bar at him, and Jaime just waves him away. He nods to the waitress, and she moves behind the bar to start pouring drinks. Jaime pours himself a drink and comes around to sit next to me.

"You're staring at that drink like it's going to tell you all the secrets of the universe." He laughs at his own joke, just like he always does. "I can tell you from experience, and from watching lots of people try that tactic... that drink won't tell you anything."

I grin and take a sip. It's smokier than I remember, but otherwise takes me back to happier days. I close my eyes and sigh until the flavor has settled on my tongue.

"I took a pro bono case," I say.

"Oh yeah?" Jaime sits beside me, staring at his drink, pretending like his ears didn't just perk up.

"It's a medical misconduct case, for a miscarriage."

"Jesus fucking—Marty, are you sure that's a good idea?"

I laugh, shrugging. "Yeah, actually. It's the best I've felt in a long time. It feels like I might actually make a difference in my client's life. I can't bring back her baby—or mine, or Brianne—but, I don't know. It feels like I'm atoning."

"Atoning for what, Marty?" He glances at me, his eyes sharp.

I shrug. My heart squeezes. I never told him about the accident, or why I was late to the hospital. I never told him how guilty I felt for being an hour away from Brianne when she lost consciousness.

Jaime shakes his head, snorting softly. "You scare me when you start saying that kind of shit, you know that?"

"Why would that scare you?"

"Because it sounds to me like you blame yourself for Brianne's passing."

"I don't."

"You shouldn't."

We both take a slow drink, and I stare at the liquid again.

"There's a new woman at work," I blurt out.

Jaime stiffens beside me, but his voice stays casual when he speaks. "Oh yeah?"

"I don't know what to think of her. She reminds me of Brianne, but different. She has that same kind of attitude, but she's..." I sigh. "I don't know. She's been through a lot. She doesn't have the carefree sort of spirit that Brianne had."

"Brianne was special."

I nod. A lump forms in my throat. "The thing is..." I sigh, shaking my head. "I don't even know why I'm telling you this."

"Because we're friends. Because you were my best man. Because you can."

I swallow and continue where I left off. "The thing is, I don't know if I'd be able to deal with Brianne's carefree positivity. This girl—this woman—that I work with, she's... *real.* She gets it." I chuckle, shaking my head. "I don't know what I'm saying. Forget it."

"It's okay to move on, Marty. Brianne would have wanted it."

My eyes prickle and the lump in my throat gets bigger. "Yeah," I croak. "It feels wrong."

Jaime is silent for a while. He nods to the girl behind the bar, and she passes over the bottle of scotch. He refills our glasses without a word, and then takes a sip.

"You know, Marty." He takes a deep breath, letting the light catch his drink. He doesn't look at me, and I'm grateful for it. "There's something I haven't told you before."

The back of my neck prickles. I turn toward him.

"What do you mean?"

"The first time Brianne went to the hospital, when I drove her—"

"And I was in the fucking mountains."

"You were at work," he corrects me, his face crumpling. "She—ah, fuck, Marty. I don't know if I should be telling you this."

"Well it's too late now." I comb my fingers through my hair in frustration. "Spit it out."

He takes a deep breath. "I think she knew something was wrong. She was white as a sheet, lying in that hospital bed. Her hand was shaking and it was so cold. I was holding it, like this." He turns his hand on the bar, palm facing up.

His voice chokes up, and he clears it with a sip of scotch.

"She told me that if anything happened to her, I had to make sure you moved on. She said—" he inhales and shakes his head. "She said that she didn't want you turning into one of the lawyers that you hate just because she was gone."

I can't look at him. My hand tightens on the glass of scotch, and I nod my head a few times.

"That's easier said than done," I finally manage to croak.

Jaime sighs. "I know. It didn't seem right to tell you before. You... you just disappeared. This is the first time I've heard you mention any other woman."

I laugh bitterly, tilting my glass back and forth to catch the light. "And I haven't even done anything. I work with her. I'm pretty sure she thinks I'm an arrogant asshole."

"Smart woman."

"Shut the fuck up." I laugh, shaking my head. Jaime grins at me, and the tension in my body dissolves a tiny bit. I take a deep, shuddering breath.

"You're not a bad person for looking at another woman."

Jaime's eyes are sharp and clear, and his voice is steady. I nod, and the guilt in my heart twists. I might not be a bad man for looking at Nicole, but I've done plenty of bad things.

I shake my head when Jaime offers to pour me another drink, lifting my car keys. "Maybe just a glass of water."

"Sure thing, buddy." He puts his hand on my shoulder and smiles at me. "It's good to see you, Marty."

"It's good to see you too. Give my best to Lauren."

Jaime nods. I have a glass of water and hang around for a few more minutes. Then, I go back to my luxurious, well-decorated, very empty house.

11

NICOLE

THE EMOTION IS OVERWHELMING when we meet with our client in the medical misconduct case. Usually I wouldn't be part of those meetings, but Martin insists that I join.

"This is as much because of you as it is because of me." He squeezes my hand as we walk toward the conference room, and velvety butterfly wings tickle my heart.

When we tell our client that not only will she get the full settlement amount, but that it will cover all her medical bills and make sure she's comfortable for many years to come, tears cloud her eyes. When I reach my hand across the table and put it on top of hers and tell her that the doctor will admit guilt, she breaks down.

My cheeks are wet, too, and I wrap her in a hug. She throws her arms around Martin, and I hold back my laughter at how awkward he looks.

When she leaves, I let out a big sigh.

"That felt good." For the first time since I've started working at Sanders & Perry, I feel like what I'm doing makes a difference. I stare after her and Martin's shoulder brushes against mine.

"It did feel good."

I turn to see Martin looking at me. He smiles, dimples and all.

"Thank you for everything."

"Just doing my job." A blush creeps over my cheeks.

"No, I mean, thank you for understanding how important this was. You put in a lot of hours." His eyes flash with pain, and I nod.

"Of course."

"You want to..." He takes a deep breath. "You want to grab dinner tonight? Assuming Carmen doesn't have you working late on other stuff."

My heart leaps in my chest.

"Well, tonight *was* a swim night," I grin. "But I can make an exception."

He nods. "Good." His movements are stiff as he walks out of the conference room. I hold back my laughter, instead taking a deep breath and gathering my things.

Did my boss just ask me out on a date?

Well, he's not really my boss. He's sort of diagonal up the food chain from me. But *still*. There's nothing wrong with a little celebratory meal with my sort-of boss, right?

I DON'T SEE Martin for the rest of the day, and by the time the office starts to empty out, I wonder if he's forgotten about me.

I go to the bathroom, even though I don't have to. I'm stalling. The office is mostly empty, and I'm done with my work for the day, but when I walked by Martin's office, it was empty.

I could text him, I guess, but that just seems a bit... desperate? Or maybe I'm just nervous and too chicken to actually do it. Maybe he changed his mind. Maybe he doesn't want to go out with me at all.

Checking my makeup in the mirror, I take a deep breath and head for the door. If he hasn't contacted me by the time I've made it to my desk, I'll go home. It's nearly seven o'clock, and that's long enough for him to make contact with me. If he doesn't want to go out to dinner with me, he should just man up and say so.

I push the door open and yelp when I see Martin leaning against the wall. He grins at me, arching his eyebrow. His suit jacket is slung over his arm, and his tie is loosened. He runs his fingers through his hair in that casual, confident, sexy movement that never fails to make me soak my underwear.

He nods. "Ready?"

"Yeah." My heart is racing and I swallow back my blush. "I'll just grab my bag."

He waits for me by the elevator, and we go down in silence. "So, where are we going?" I ask as the elevator whirrs downward. He glances at me, grinning.

"It's a surprise."

"Of course it is."

"What's that supposed to mean?"

"You wouldn't just ask me out to a normal dinner, would you? It would have to be some big shot dinner."

He laughs, and my heart melts. I wish he laughed more often; his smile is staggering.

"What's a big shot dinner?"

"You know, a big surprise, and something with the words 'degustation' in it, with like, two peas and a little lump of liver or something."

"You don't like liver?"

I roll my eyes. "Come on, Big Shot. Where are we going?"

"What if I was actually taking you to McDonalds? Then how would you feel?"

"I'd be waiting for my stomach ache and McHangover from eating fast food," I laugh. The elevator opens and he gestures to let me go ahead of him.

"Wow," I grin. "What a gentleman. Didn't know you had it in you."

"I'm not that bad, am I?"

"The first time I met you, you confronted me about taking a parking space that was rightfully mine."

"That's debatable."

I laugh, shaking my head. "You're never going to let that go, are you?"

A smile plays on his lips and I nudge him with my shoulder. "I'll admit, I did see a new side of you during the pro bono case."

"Yeah?" He pulls his car keys out of his pocket. Glancing at me, he nods toward his car. "What side is that?"

"A human side."

Martin chuckles and his car beeps as he unlocks it. "You don't think I'm human?"

"You're like a buff, swim team, robo-lawyer."

I open the passenger's side door as he glances at me over the roof of the car. His eyes glimmer. "You think I'm buff?"

My cheeks flush and I roll my eyes to hide it. "Please. Like you don't already know. I bet your house is just one big mirror so you can check yourself out all the time."

He laughs, and the butterflies tickle my heart again. We get in the car and he grins at me.

"I'm guessing you missed the robo-lawyer part of that." I click my seatbelt, glancing at him sideways. "Figures you'd focus on the compliments."

"I didn't miss any of it."

We drive in silence for a few minutes. The sun has gone down, as it usually has when I leave work. Being driven through the city in a BMW is a different experience than fighting with traffic in my old beater, though. We drive in silence until Martin pulls in beside a little restaurant.

"You like sushi?"

I grin. "That's a bit of a risk, isn't it? What if I said no?"

"Who doesn't like sushi?"

"Some people don't like the idea of eating raw fish."

He frowns, genuinely confused, and I laugh.

"You're lucky, though. I love sushi. Good choice."

We walk into the restaurant, and Martin threads his fingers through mine. Heat zips down my spine and my cheeks flush again. His hand feels warm and strong, and I lean slightly into his body. It's natural to hold his hand like this, like it's us against the world.

We're brought to a table in the back corner and Martin releases my hand to sit down. A spark of disappointment goes through me and I shake my head to dispel it. I sit down across from him. His angular face is lit up by the flickering candle on the table, and he smiles at me.

"Well, I haven't done this in a long time." He rubs his jaw, chuckling. A thin layer of stubble covers his face, and I wonder what it would feel like to run my fingers over it.

"Right there with you," I laugh. "I'm not sure whether I'm loving it or supremely uncomfortable."

"You sure do know how to stroke a man's ego." His eyes flash as he grins at me. "Just throwing out compliments all over the place."

"Your ego doesn't need any stroking."

His lips drop open and he holds my gaze for a few moments. An immature joke about 'stroking' goes through my head, but I resist the urge to say it. It doesn't feel like the right time. It feels like if I said it, it wouldn't come out as a joke at all.

The waiter comes back with menus and a little piece of paper to mark down our choices. Martin takes it with a nod and I look at him over my menu.

"If you're intending on ordering for me, you better think again." I take the little slip of paper from his hands. "No man orders for me, ever."

"I ordered Chinese for you the other night."

My cheeks flush when my thoughts flick to that moment in his office. I shrug. "First time for everything."

"There certainly is." His eyes drop to my lips, and my heart beats harder. I try to focus on the menu, but the heat flooding through my body is making it hard to think about anything except his lips, his eyes, and his broad, strong hands.

12

MARTIN

I COULD LIE to myself and say that this is just a business dinner. I could say that it's a celebratory meal after a hard-won case with lots of emotional baggage.

That's not true, though.

I'm here because of Nicole. I'm here to be with her. Being alone with her is exhilarating. I shift in my seat, stealing a glance at her. She's grabbed the little pencil and is marking down what she wants on our strip of paper.

"You feeding the entire city with that order?"

She pauses, glancing at me with her eyes wide. "Wait... you're paying, right?"

I'm still trying to work out whether she's joking or not when she bursts out laughing. I shake my head.

"You never cease to surprise me." I arch an eyebrow at her.

"With my wit and charm?"

"With your impertinence."

"Impertinence!" The pencil hovers above the sheet as she stares at me, wide-eyed. A grin twitches at her lips and she shakes her head. "You are something else, Mr. Big Shot."

"I'll take that as a compliment."

"You would."

She marks down another item on the sheet, and then glances up at me. "Wouldn't want to go hungry."

I grin, taking the sheet from her and looking over her choices. My eyebrows arch and I nod.

"There are some good choices here."

"Don't sound so surprised."

"I'll just add the dragon roll," I say, taking the pencil from her hands. "It's the best one on the menu."

The waiter collects our order and brings us a pot of tea. I lift my cup up and touch it to Nicole's. "Cheers."

She smiles at me, and a bolt of lightning goes down my spine. How does she do that? With one look, she makes me forget about everything except how badly I want to fuck her senseless. Resisting that is wearing me down.

Nicole puts her teacup down and folds her hands on the table, leaning toward me. "So, Martin." She leans in. "What's this all about?"

"What's what all about?"

She waves her hand. "This. This dinner. This... date?" Her eyebrows lift. "Last time I checked, you were standing in front of my car telling me that we had to keep it professional."

"This is professional."

"Uh-huh."

I grin. "Totally professional. We're just having a celebratory meal after a tough case."

"Right."

"Right."

She sighs, shaking her head. "I can't believe you have the nerve to call *me* impertinent."

I laugh and lean back in my chair. "Can't I just take you out for a nice meal? Why does it have to mean anything?"

"Because I haven't been out with a man since Jack died," she blurts out. Her cheeks flush and she looks down at her hands. I watch her chest rise and fall, and she finally lifts her eyes back to me.

She smiles shyly. "Pathetic, isn't it?"

"How is that pathetic?" My voice is soft. I reach across the table and put my hands on top of hers. She threads her fingers through mine and I take a deep breath. "To tell you the truth, this is the first time I've been out with a woman since Brianne died, too."

"Really?"

I sigh, nodding. "Yeah."

"That surprises me," she admits.

"Why?"

Her hands tighten in mine, and she stares at them. She grins, shaking her head. "I guess I just thought you were some fancy lawyer, with more money than you knew what to do with and more women than you could keep track of."

I laugh, shaking my head. "You've been at the office with me most evenings until eight or nine. When would I have time to lose track of all these women?"

A blush stains her cheeks. Her eyes flick up to mine, and she tucks a strand of dark hair behind her ear. The waiter appears with our first round of sushi, and Nicole's eyes brighten. She smiles at the waiter and then grabs her chopsticks.

"You're not so bad, you know." She plucks a roll from the plate.

"Gee, thanks," I grin. "Please, don't flatter me too much. It might go to my head."

"I know. That's why I'm being very diplomatic about it. You can never be too careful."

I laugh and shake my head. We eat in silence for a few

minutes. Every time Nicole opens her mouth to eat a piece of sushi, I practically lose control. Images flood my brain of all the other things that would make Nicole open her mouth like that. I clear my throat and shift in my seat, then grab my cup of tea and take a sip.

We fall into easy conversation. Nicole tells me that she has a sister, and I tell her I'm an only child.

"That explains a lot."

I decide to let that slide.

We talk about our childhood and various cases at work. We avoid the big elephant in the room, which is the fact that we've both been widowed. It doesn't feel like the right time to bring it up.

We walk hand-in-hand back to the car, and I drive us back to Nicole's car at the office. I park next to her and get out, opening her door for her. She smiles at me, her eyebrows arching.

"Wow, you *are* a gentleman. This is a new side of you."

"I'm not that bad." I grin, taking a step toward her.

"No, you're not."

We stand in front of each other in the deserted parking lot. Her eyes sparkle. Her chest moves with every breath, and my heartbeat rushes in my ears. I put my hand on her hip, and she closes her eyes for a second. She places her hands on my chest, inching them up toward my neck.

We move slowly, tentatively. Her scent fills my nostrils and desire floods through my veins. I use my other hand to tilt her chin up, and then I lower my lips to hers. It happens slowly, as if neither of us is quite sure what to do.

Her lips are soft; her kiss is tender. She wraps her arms around my neck and deepens the kiss. My hands drift to her lower back and I pull her closer. My lips explore hers. My tongue teases her mouth open, and I nip her lower lip with my teeth.

She moans into my mouth and then kisses me harder. I back her up against her car, pressing the length of my body against hers. She crushes her lips against mine, moaning softly as her hands tangle into my hair. Her shirt is tucked into her skirt, and I pull it up to run my hands on her bare skin.

She moans again, rolling her hips toward me. We're panting, touching, kissing. My movements become faster as my hands claw at her body. I cup her breast, moaning as I run my teeth along her lower lip. I press my hard cock against her stomach and she gasps, throwing her head back.

I kiss her jaw, her neck, her collarbone. It's frantic. It's intense. It's everything I've ever wanted. And then, as soon as it started, Nicole's hands are on my chest and she's pushing me away.

"Stop, stop." She pants, turning her head away from me. "Please."

"Sorry." I stop immediately. Her breaths are short and she squeezes her eyes shut. Worry worms itself into my heart and I take a step back. I frown. "Sorry, Nicole. I didn't... are you okay?"

"I'm fine," she says, finally looking at me. "Sorry. That's the first...." She takes a deep breath, shaking her head. "It was just so intense. I freaked out. I haven't..."

"I get it."

She looks at me, her eyebrows arched in concern. She bites her lip and I take her hand in mine.

We say nothing for a few seconds. She squeezes my hand and takes a deep breath.

"I should probably head home. Early morning tomorrow."

My throat tightens. I nod. “Of course. Me too.”

“Thank you for dinner. It was lovely, and you’re… you’re alright.”

“I’m alright?” I grin, tucking a strand of her hair behind her ear.

“Yeah.”

“That might be the best compliment anyone’s ever given me.”

She laughs, leaning into my hand as I cup her cheek. Then, she takes a deep breath and nods to her car. “I’ll see you tomorrow.”

“See you tomorrow.”

She puts a hand on my shoulder and brushes her lips against my cheek.

I watch her drive away and then blow all the air out of my lungs. I slide into the driver’s seat and stare out the windshield, seeing nothing. My body is still buzzing, but my mind is spinning in the opposite direction. I feel like I crossed a line.

We got carried away. We shouldn’t have done that. *I* shouldn’t have done that.

13

NICOLE

I FLOP down in my bed and groan. My palms fly to my face and I roll over onto my side, groaning louder. The whole drive home was a blur, and now I'm just replaying the kiss in my head over and over.

And over.

And over.

My whole body is still buzzing. Every time I think about his hands on my skin, the way he ripped my shirt out from my skirt, I groan again.

Why did I stop him?

Maybe he would have bent me over the hood of his car right then and there. I squeeze my eyes shut. I could feel his hard length pressing into my stomach when he pushed me up against the car. I take a deep breath and groan again.

I was so turned on. I'm still turned on! I want him—I know I do. So why did I freak out? That was the craziest kiss and I ruined it.

I have to go back into work tomorrow knowing that we did that. Knowing that I stopped it!

Pushing myself off the bed, I go to the kitchen to get a glass of water. I gulp it down and then grab my phone. Should I text him?

I snort at the thought. What would I even say?

My phone ringing startles me. I take a deep breath when my sister's name pops up on the screen.

"Hey, Jenna."

"Nic! I haven't heard from you all week. How is work going?"

"Work is good." I run my finger along the edge of my glass. "You know, busy. The usual."

I cringe. I shouldn't have kissed him, but I liked it.

Jenna makes a noise. "Look, I wanted to talk to you because Gabby's birthday is coming up. I was thinking of having a family dinner on Saturday if you're free? Nothing too crazy, just us and you and a birthday cake.

"Sure, sounds good," I say as I walk back toward the bedroom. "What time?"

"Five o'clock?"

I chuckle. "I ate dinner at almost nine tonight. Five is practically lunchtime."

"Try having kids," she laughs. A jolt passes through my heart. I was supposed to have a baby by now, but then the accident happened.

Jenna sense my mood. "Sorry."

"It's okay," I say. "I'll see you Saturday."

"Get some sleep."

"Okay, Mom."

She laughs. "Someone needs to take care of you."

We hang up the phone and I lie back down in bed. Someone *does* need to take care of me. Today, it felt like Martin was the one to do it. He could have taken care of me, right there in the parking lot. My hand drifts down to my mound and I take a deep breath.

But... it's wrong. He's practically my boss. If anyone were to find out, I could lose my job. He certainly wouldn't, he's a partner at the firm. But me?

I'd be right back where I started, with no money, no job, no insurance payment, and a whole heap of medical bills.

On cue, my side starts to ache. I rummage through the medicine cabinet and find some painkillers, and then get ready for bed.

Alone, as usual.

WHEN I GET to work in the morning, the nervousness inside me is still there. I glance down the hallway toward Martin's office and then sit down at my desk. I think I slept funny because my back is aching—but maybe it's just nerves. My pain seems to get worse when I'm stressed.

I glance at the clock—just after 7 a.m. With a deep breath, I turn on my computer and open the files for one of Carmen's cases. She needs me to do a lot of filing today, which is mindless and tedious, and gives me a lot of time to think about last night on repeat.

I know I'll be imagining the kiss over, and over, and over...

After only a few minutes, I blow the air out of my lungs and stand up. I need a coffee.

I take the long way around to the kitchen, just to walk by Martin's office. The light is on—of course it is, he's always one of the first ones here.

My hands tremble as I make a coffee. I hesitate, then say 'fuck it' under my breath and make another one. The two mugs steam, and coffee sloshes back and forth as I walk toward Martin's office.

Call it a peace offering—or maybe just an excuse to see him. I wonder if he knows how good he looks in a suit.

Of course he does. He's Martin Henderson. He wouldn't be buying expensive, perfectly-tailored suits if he didn't know how good he looked in them... and how much it makes me want to rip them off.

The door is closed, so I set one of the mugs on the ground and knock.

"Come in," his deep growl comes through the door. Heat pools between my legs. I turn the knob and pick up the cup of coffee, kicking the door closed behind me.

I lift the cups. "Coffee?"

He's going over a big stack of files. He glances up and his face softens. He nods.

"Thanks."

I walk forward and put the mug down on his desk. He thanks me again and takes a sip. We look at each other for a few moments. I shift from foot to foot, running my finger along the edge of my mug.

"Look, Martin, about last night—"

"Don't mention it. It was inappropriate."

My mouth is still open so I close it. I nod.

"Yeah."

His eyes are burning a hole through me. We stare at each other for a long moment, and then he stands up from his chair. My heart starts beating faster as he comes around toward me. He takes the mug out of my hands and places it next to his on the desk.

I watch him, immobile. He takes a deep breath, looking at my pencil skirt, and my shirt. His hand drifts up the buttons that line the front and he touches my jaw with the backs of his fingers. He runs his hand back to my hair, tilting my chin up toward him.

"Why are you here?"

I falter. "I brought you coffee."

"Is that all?" He brings his other hand up and runs his thumb across my lower lip. I part my lips and my breath hitches at the touch. My legs are shaking. He slides his thumb between my lips and I close my eyes, sucking it gently. He exhales, pulling it out again. When he slides it back in again, I roll my tongue over the tip of it. He groans. His fingers curl into the nape of my neck and he slides his thumb in and out of my mouth once more.

"I don't think you're here to bring me coffee," he growls.

I whimper.

"I think you're here because you haven't been able to stop thinking about last night." He backs me up so that my ass presses up against his desk. His hand is still holding my head tilted up toward him, and he trails his thumb from my lips down to my chin.

"I think you went home and thought of me," he says in a low voice. His thigh nestles between mine, and I know he can feel the heat emanating from my core.

He parts my lips with his thumb. Slowly, torturously, he slides his thumb between my lips again. He dips his head down so his breath tickles my ear. His big, muscular body cages me against the desk.

"I think you masturbated to the thought of me." Thumb in, and out, and in. "I think you wish that was my cock."

I moan.

He drops his hand from my chin and moves it to my thigh, tugging my pencil skirt up around my hips.

"See, I think you want something else," he growls, his lips close to mine. His foot kicks my legs apart and he presses me up against the desk. With his hand behind my neck and his body pinning me against his desk, I can't move. Not that I'd want to.

My whole body is on fire. My heart is hammering in my chest and I whimper when he moves his hand between my legs. He runs his fingers over the thin fabric of my panties. My breath is ragged and I roll my hips toward him.

"See?" He grins. "I know what you want."

His lips brush against mine as gently as his fingers touch my underwear. He kisses me harder, sliding his fingers along the edge of my panties. My legs tremble. His grip on the nape of my neck tightens.

His fingers slide underneath my panties and he growls when he feels my slit.

"You're soaking wet."

"I know."

His thick, strong fingers start sliding back and forth, teasing my opening and just brushing my bud. I'm panting now. His body presses into mine, making me lean back against the desk. His fingers move a little harder as he keeps his face close to mine. I can feel his hot breath washing over me as his hand sends waves of pleasure through my whole body.

"Anyone could walk in," I pant, not really caring about it at all.

"Well, you'd better hurry up and come, then." He lifts his hand up to his lips and tastes my honey. He closes his eyes and groans. "I've been wanting to taste you since the moment I laid eyes on you."

I exhale at his words, and he pulls my head back. He kisses my neck, returning his fingers back to my sopping wet slit. When he slides his fingers inside me, I gasp. He curls them just the right way, driving them in and out of me as his thumb brushes against my clit.

My head is spinning. My whole body is on fire. He growls next to my ear, running his tongue up the side of my neck. It might be the fact that a man hasn't touched me in a very long time, but it feels like more than that.

He's got total control over me right now. I'm his, completely. He tilts my head back and crushes his lips against mine as his fingers find that spot on the front of my walls. He grins as my body jumps in his hands. I moan again, burying my face in his neck. I bite down on his suit jacket, moaning louder.

His hand moves faster and I'm getting closer to the edge. He drops his hand from the back of my neck and leans me back, popping open the buttons of my blouse in a swift movement. With his fingers buried deep inside me and his thumb twirling around my clit, he rips my bra down and cups my breasts. I lean back on the desk and hear papers falling to the ground, but I don't care.

His head dips down and he takes my breast in his mouth.

My back arches, my legs shake, and my mouth drops open in a silent scream.

"That's it, angel," he growls, teasing my nipples. "Come for me. Come right here on my desk like that bad girl you are."

He drives his fingers deeper and they make a wet, slurping sound that vaguely registers in my mind. I can't think straight, because all I can focus on is the heat between my legs and my inability to hold myself up.

I fly over the edge as Martin's deep growl urges me onward. "Come all over my hands, angel. Soak through those dirty little panties of yours."

He pulls me to him and crushes his lips against mine, and I'm done. I shake in his arms, holding onto him for dear life as I come over and over and over onto his fingers.

When it's over, I stare at him, panting. He looks at me, with my blouse ripped open and my bra pulled off my breasts. He stares at my skirt bunched up around my hips and shakes his head.

"You're fucking gorgeous," he says. "Do you know that?"

14

MARTIN

I GENTLY REPLACE Nicole's underwear and pull her skirt down over her legs. She leans into me, laying a soft kiss on my lips. Her hands drift downward and she feels the rock-hard erection tenting my pants. I pull her hands away, shaking my head.

"Uh-uh," I sigh. "Not yet."

"That's not fair."

"Greedy girl," I grin, smacking her ass. I kiss her, and the feeling of her breasts pressed up against me sends another rush of blood between my legs.

"I want you to feel like I do," she says, reaching for my pants again. "I... I don't know why I stopped yesterday."

I grab her wrists with one hand and spin her around. I use my other arm to pull her body into mine and press my erection into her ass.

"You'll get it soon enough," I growl. "But I'm going to make you wait."

"Why?" Nicole's eyes are closed as she leans her head back into me. Her blouse is still open, and I let my fingers drift over her breasts. She shivers.

"I want to enjoy every second of this," I say. "First, I'll make you come again with my hands." I tighten my hold on her wrists and run my other hand up toward her neck. "And then my mouth." I kiss the sensitive skin below her ear. "And then my cock." She whimpers when I press my length against her ass. "And I want to take my time. I'm not going to bend you over and fuck you on this desk. Not yet."

"What if I want you to?"

"Well, you're just going to have to be patient." I let go of her wrists and turn her back around toward me. I kiss her softly, and then start buttoning her blouse again. "Better get dressed, people will be arriving at the office soon."

Nicole stares at me, wide-eyed, as she buttons her blouse. I watch her straighten her clothes and tie her hair back. She looks at my desk and grabs her cup of coffee, grimacing when she takes a sip.

"Cold."

"Wonder why that is."

She laughs, shaking her head. "You know, I did just come in here to bring you a cup of coffee as a peace offering. I didn't think..."

I run my fingers along her jaw and kiss her again. "I dreamt of you all night," I growl. "I knew that I wouldn't be able to keep my hands off you when I saw you again."

She sighs, closing her eyes and leaning her forehead against mine.

"What happened to being inappropriate? This hardly constitutes professional conduct." She grins at me.

I shrug. "I'm only human."

"I liked..." She blushes. My cock throbs. "I liked it. You... What you did."

"I know you did." Her pupils dilate and my cock throbs.

She fucking loved every second of it. "I know what you like, Nicole. I'm sick of holding back."

She nods, and her eyes linger on mine. Then she turns and straightens her shoulders before walking out the door. I hear Kelly's surprised greeting and Nicole's over-enthusiastic response. I grin and turn to the mess of papers on my desk and the floor.

I DON'T SEE Nicole for the rest of the day, and I do my best to focus on work. Once in a while, though, I think of the way she looked with her skirt up near her waist. I think of the face she made when she came, and how she bit into my shoulder to stifle her scream.

I never knew working late was a perk until Nicole slips into my office around nine o'clock.

"Hey." She leans against the door as a blush creeps up her cheeks. "You miss me?"

"Terribly."

I stand up, and she locks the door. There's no preamble, no wasting any time. The instant the door is locked, my arms are around her and I'm devouring her. She reaches for my belt buckle and I tsk.

"What did I tell you this morning?"

"Martin—"

I put my fingers to her lips and she pouts. I guide her toward the couch.

"I told you I was going to take my time," I growl. She bites her lip, and I wonder if I'll even be able to hold back. I sit down on the couch in front of her.

"Take off your clothes. Let me see you."

Her eyes widen and a flush creeps over her cheeks. Then, without a word, she starts unbuttoning her blouse, one button at a time. I groan and my eyes lower with her fingers. She slips the blouse off her shoulders and lays it on a chair. Then, she unzips her skirt and slips it off. She starts taking off her shoes but I stop her.

"Keep them on," I growl. She bites her lip and nods.

"Yes, sir."

I groan. "I like when you talk to me like that."

She takes a step toward me and I lean forward, running my hands up her legs. Her panties are the same color as her bra—white with delicate lace on the edges.

"You like when I call you 'sir'?"

I nod and she turns around for me. I run my hands over her ass and she looks at me over her shoulder.

"Mr. Big Shot likes to be in control."

I smack her ass. "Maybe I do."

"Well, what do you want me to do?"

My cock throbs. She looks at me, fluttering those long lashes at me. Her hands run up her arms and she lets her bra straps fall off her shoulders. I watch, entranced, as she unclasps her bra and tosses it toward the chair with her other clothing.

"Show me your pussy."

She bites her lip again, and I exhale slowly. I've hardly touched her and I feel like I'm going to explode. She hooks her fingers into her panties and drops them to the ground, kicking them aside with her tall black stilettos.

I can't resist any more. I growl, pulling her toward me. I drag my fingers through her slit and gasp at her wetness. She straddles me on the couch, grinding her naked body on top of mine. My hands run over her body, touching and tugging and feeling and grabbing. I reach between her legs and she gasps when I slide two fingers deep inside her.

Then, she rocks her hips back and forth and fucks my

hand. She lets out little moans as I curl my fingers inside her, reaching deep for her most sensitive spot.

"Come all over my hand, baby girl," I growl. "Make a mess of my pants. I want you to come all over me."

She gasps, moaning again as she rides me. With one hand still inside her, I reach back and smack her ass with a loud clap. She yelps, falling into me and pressing her breasts into my face. She rides my hand harder as I suck her tits until I feel her come all over me.

I moan with her, loving the way her body is contracting and convulsing on top of me. When she lets out a long moan and falls quiet, I groan and slip my fingers out of her.

"Martin—" she gasps. Before she can speak, I hook my arms under her thighs and lift her up. She gasps.

"Sit on my fucking face, angel," I growl. She lets out a loud moan when my mouth connects with her clit.

15

NICOLE

I DIDN'T THINK Martin was serious when he said he'd make me wait. But when a second orgasm washes over me as I quiver on his face, I know he meant it.

He growls, lowering me down and holding me close to his chest.

"Mmm," he says, licking his lips. "You taste so fucking good."

I blush. "You think so?"

"Fucking right I do."

There's a primal, animalistic look in his eyes that turns me on like never before. He runs his hands down my body. He cups my ass and gives it a squeeze. I straddle him, toying with the buttons of his shirt.

"You're still wearing all your clothes. That hardly seems fair."

"You're still wearing your shoes," he grins.

"Only because you told me to."

He reaches up and starts unbuttoning his shirt. My hands push the shirt open, and I sigh as I run my fingers across his chest. He's got a swimmer's body—broad in the shoulders and back, tapering down to a slim waist. I pull his shirt out of his pants and open it, running my hands all over his stomach.

"I like your body."

"Me too," he replies, giving my ass a light smack.

"You like my body or your own?" I grin, and he flips me over onto my back beside him.

"Why not both?"

I laugh, and he crushes his lips to mine. In a flash, he's taking his shirt off and unbuckling his pants. I bite my lip, watching him.

Something inside me starts to wake up. This desire, deep in the pit of my stomach—it feels unfamiliar. It feels *good*. I thought it died with Jack, but seeing Martin here—in all his manly, muscled glory—makes me remember what it feels like to be a woman. His eyes roam all over my body and he shakes his head.

"You look incredible."

"You look okay."

He grins. "Still impertinent."

"Still an asshole."

With one movement, he flips me over and smacks my ass.

"Bad girl."

"For calling you an asshole?"

He smacks my ass again, harder. I gasp as the pain dissolves into pleasure. Wetness gathers between my legs. I glance over my shoulder at him.

He turns me around so I'm on my back again. I run my fingers over his biceps, his shoulders, and down toward his cock.

He spreads my legs and lets out a sigh. His cock is straining against his underwear, and he slides it down his muscular legs. A look crosses his face and he glances toward his desk. He frowns.

"You, uh... you got any condoms?"

My eyebrows arch and I bite my lip. I shake my head.

"I haven't carried condoms with me in... jeez. Since before Jack."

Martin sits down on the couch at my feet, chuckling. "Me neither."

I prop myself up onto my elbows and sigh. "We're amateurs."

"Rookies."

His cock is still rock hard, resting against his stomach. I sit up and run my fingers up his shaft. He groans, closing his eyes.

"You don't have to do that, Nicole."

"Do what?" I wrap my fingers around his shaft and he exhales slowly.

"I mean, if you don't want to."

"I want to."

He sighs again, leaning back on the sofa. He puts one arm around me as I stroke him. His skin feels soft and warm to the touch, and his cock jumps in my hand every few seconds. I watch it get harder as I touch it. I move my hand faster and he groans louder. It feels so—I don't know, powerful? —to be here like this. It's my touch that's making him feel this way, and it's my touch that will send him over the edge.

He opens his eyes and stares at me. He runs his fingers through my hair and I press my body close to his. In a way, this feels more intimate than if he was inside me. He stares into my eyes as I stroke his cock, and then he closes them and moans.

When he comes, it sends a thrill shivering all the way

down my spine. His whole body tenses. The muscles in his neck bulge and his jaw clenches until he lets out a long, low growl. His cock gets harder, its head a deep shade of purple.

I watch, fascinated. It's like I'd forgotten what it was like, to be with a man. He shoots ropes of white seed as he groans, trembling and convulsing on the couch. We make a mess all over his stomach, his chest, my hand, my breasts. It goes everywhere. He keeps his arm around me, panting. Neither of us moves for a few moments as he catches his breath.

"Messy," I say, trailing my fingers through the sticky seed on his stomach.

"Look what you did to me."

"What you did to yourself," I grin. He tucks a strand of hair behind my ear and sighs again.

"That felt so fucking good."

"Yeah."

We sit there for a few seconds, and then the mess starts to drip down the sides of his abdomen. He peels himself off the couch and grabs some tissues. I giggle and Martin shakes his head.

"It's everywhere."

"When was the last time you masturbated? There's so much of it."

"This morning," he says, glancing at me. He grins. A blush creeps over my cheeks and I bite my lip.

When we're cleaned up and clothed again, we sit down on the couch. I lay my head on his shoulder and sigh in contentment.

"We probably shouldn't leave together every evening," he says slowly.

I sigh and nod. "I know."

"I don't think Carmen would be too happy about this."

"I can't lose this job."

Martin tightens his arm around my shoulders and kisses the top of my head. "You won't get fired."

"No, *you* won't get fired," I laugh. "I'm just a lowly paralegal who started here a couple months ago. I know where I stand."

He runs his fingers along my cheek and stares into my eyes. He smiles and shakes his head.

"I don't think you do."

My heart thumps, and I don't know how to respond.

He opens his mouth and then closes it again, and finally smiles at me. "You hungry? We could grab some dinner."

I laugh. "I thought we weren't supposed to leave the office together."

"Fuck it." He stands and helps me up off the couch. I put my hand on his arm and look up at him, my eyebrows drawing together.

"Martin, I meant what I said before. I can't lose this job. I have so much medical debt it makes my head spin."

"Still no payout from the life insurance?"

I sigh and shake my head. "They keep just telling me they're reviewing it, but it's been over a year."

He wraps his arms around me and kisses my forehead.

"I'll make sure you don't lose your job, Nicole. Do you want me to ask a friend of mine that specializes in insurance cases? He's at another firm—we went to law school together. He owes me a favor."

"You'd do that?"

His eyes soften and he kisses me gently. "Yes, I would."

My knees go weak. When I look at Martin, it's a weird mix of excitement, lust, and guilt that fills me. I'm not sure if I'm ready to jump into anything serious... but I think it might be too late.

So, I just nod my head. "Okay."

He smiles. "Let's get some dinner."

For the second night in the row, we leave the office together. I'll be honest, though, I don't care one bit if anyone sees us. I'm too busy falling for my very attractive, very emotionally unavailable boss.

16

MARTIN

April runs into May, and I run into Nicole. Full speed, without reserve, I crash into her like a runaway train. Once I taste her, there's no stopping me. We have sex in my office, at her house, at my house, in the office bathrooms—wherever we can get our hands on each other. In between sweaty, intense sex, we lay quietly and let our broken hearts feel the balm of human company.

As the weather starts to warm up, so does my heart. Day by day, the armor I've put up starts to crumble. It happens in small moments, almost imperceptibly. When Nicole slips her hand into mine as we walk on the street, a piece of my anger falls away. When she calls me Big Shot, when she kisses the tip of my nose. Her warmth softens my edges and wakes up a piece of me that I thought died with Brianne.

There are whispers about Nicole and me, but no one confronts me. I see the way people look at us whenever we talk at work, and I know that people have seen us spend more and more time together. I think they might be more surprised to see me laughing and smiling than anything. My smiles have been few and far between lately.

It feels like I'm finally crawling out of a dark hole that has engulfed me for the past year. When I'm with Nicole, I feel good, and I start craving that feeling. I start craving *her*.

She's like a drug to me, and I'm nothing but a junkie.

After a couple weeks, on a Friday, I send her a text to meet me at our favorite sushi restaurant after work. I count down the minutes until then. I can't keep the smile off my face. Finally, I finish my work for the day and head for the elevator.

I get to the restaurant before her, but I don't have to wait long. She's changed out of her work clothes and is dressed exactly how I like her—tight jeans and a simple white tee shirt. Her hair is down, falling just past her shoulders. When she sees me, a big smile breaks across her face.

She puts her arm around my neck and kisses me, and she smells just as good as ever. I motion to sit down. She grabs the pencil and paper to mark down our order, grinning at me.

"I see you left this blank, for once."

"I trust you to choose."

"Finally." She lets out an exaggerated sigh, rolling her eyes. The walls around my heart crumble a little bit more. "It only took a month and a half."

"Hey, so, I was wondering—since we both just finished up a couple big cases and we have the weekend off, how do you feel about going away?"

Her eyes widen. She smiles, and a bolt of lightning goes through my chest.

"You want to have a weekend away?"

"Just you and me."

She bites her lip, smiling. "Yeah, I'd like that."

"Good."

Her eyes linger on mine and her smile widens.

"What?"

She laughs, shaking her head. "You just... I was wrong about you, Marty."

"I'm not an arrogant ass?"

"Well, not all the time." She winks at me. "No, you're okay. You're actually pretty romantic."

"Maybe you make me that way."

She doesn't answer, but her eyes soften and her smile widens. My heart thumps, and I wonder how it's possible that I got so lucky. This feels like not only did I get blessed with Brianne, but I've been blessed a second time. Nicole gets me in a way that no one else has been able to. She understands both the darkness and the light inside me, and she accepts me for it. She might even love me for it.

We eat more food than we should, and Nicole pushes her plate away, rubbing her belly.

"Are you trying to fatten me up?"

"I was going to ask you the same thing," I say, plucking the last piece of nigiri off the plate.

We walk out of the restaurant and I squeeze her hand. "How do you feel about meeting one of my good friends? He owns a bar not far from here."

Her eyebrows arch. "You have friends?"

I grin and nudge her with my elbow. "Don't be so smart, it doesn't suit you."

"It was an honest question." She squeezes my hand, laughing. Her grey eyes have little flecks of green on the edges, and right now her eyes look like they're studded with emeralds.

"He and I went to college together."

She leans her head against my shoulder and I put my arm around her. We walk to my car and she sighs.

"What's that big sigh about?" I open the passenger's side door for her, and she puts her hand on top of it, staring at me.

"I'm just... happy." Her smile is more tentative this time, and a blush warms her cheeks. I lean over the door and kiss her.

"So am I."

I CAN TELL RIGHT AWAY that Jaime likes Nicole. They laugh together, give me shit for being a hotshot lawyer, and we spend the evening hanging out. When Nicole goes to the bathroom, Jaime raises his eyebrows at me.

"Is this the girl you were talking about before? The one you work with?"

I nod.

He whistles and shakes his head. "You have some fucking luck with women, buddy," he laughs. "I don't know how you do it."

"What's that supposed to mean?" I grin.

"No one wins the lottery twice."

Nicole comes back toward us and warmth radiates through my chest. She slides her hand over my thigh when she sits down, and suddenly it feels like it's time to go home. When she looks at me, I can tell she's thinking the same thing. The air between us crackles with heat, and I nod to Jaime.

"See you next week."

"Alright."

Then, I take Nicole home and we get tangled in the bedsheets together.

THE NEXT MORNING, we stop at her place to get a change of clothes. I've rented a cabin near Bighorn Park, about an hour and a half west of Denver. The thought of escaping the city and being in the wilderness with Nicole sounds like heaven. Getting there, on the other hand, is more of a struggle.

We'll have to pass right by the spot where I had an accident on my way back to see Brianne in the hospital. I smashed the front of my car into someone, but I was in such a panic to be by her side that I drove off. My wife was unconscious, miscarrying our first child, and I was reckless with worry.

By the time I got to her in the hospital, she was already in surgery. I never got to say goodbye. If I hadn't gotten into that accident, if I hadn't been in the mountains for a case...

I sigh. I'm going to have to get over this at some point. With Nicole by my side, it finally feels like I might be able to.

When we get on the highway, Nicole falls silent. Her grip tightens on the car door, and I see tension rippling in her jaw.

"You okay?"

She nods but says nothing. Her neck pulses with every heartbeat. She turns her head and looks out the window, her breath shallow.

Maybe she's just sensing what I feel. We're about ten minutes away from the spot where I crashed. Guilt gnaws at my stomach when I think of the other car. I remember looking in my rear-view mirror and seeing them sliding toward the ditch on the opposite side of the road.

Knowing what I know now, that I was too late for Brianne, I would have stopped. I *should* have stopped either way. It's the single most awful thing I've ever done, not to mention completely illegal.

I take a deep breath and tighten my grip on the steering wheel.

I drove back past the spot the next day, and the car was gone. That means they were okay, doesn't it? They must have driven off or been towed. My mind relives that moment a thousand times as we get closer to the accident.

I should have stopped.

In a few minutes, we'll be past the scene of my accident. Past the scene of my crime. Past my shame, and my guilt, and the single worst deed of my miserable existence. I'll drive past it, and I'll be able to enjoy the weekend with the beautiful woman sitting beside me.

But then, Nicole takes a deep breath.

"Do you mind pulling over just up here?"

"What? Why?" My heart thunders. My jaw ticks as I try to control the uncontrollable beating in my chest. My vision starts to tunnel, and I take slow, quiet breaths through my nose.

"Just... please? I'll show you the spot."

I frown, and the blood drains from my face. Nicole shifts in her seat. She points to a spot on the side of the road, and my mouth goes dry.

"Pull over up here."

I can't speak. The awful, horrible, earth-shattering truth dawns on me. Nicole stares out the window for a few excruciating seconds, and then she takes a deep breath.

"This is where Jack died." The truth hits me in the face like a sledgehammer. The world tilts on its axis and I feel like I'm going to throw up. "We were side-swiped by a speeding car and spun twice. We hit that tree." She points to a huge pine tree by the side of the road. She unbuckles her seatbelt and opens the door, finally glancing at me.

"I know it's morbid, but do you mind if we just have a moment here?"

I clear my throat, forcing myself to meet her eye.

"Sure. Of course."

17

NICOLE

I HAVEN'T BEEN BACK HERE since the day of the accident. It's been almost a year and a half, but it feels as raw as if it happened yesterday. For the first time in a couple months, my side throbs and my back aches. Emotion swirls inside me, thick and black and confusing. I step outside. Fresh mountain air whips around me, stinging my eyes and drawing out the tears that I've been trying to hold back.

I wasn't going to say anything. I was going to let Martin drive by, but as we got closer, I knew I had to pay my respects. My feet crunch on a thin layer of gravel on the side of the road. The ditch is shallow, but I'm still careful as I make my way down toward the tree.

The tree. The tree that featured in my nightmares for weeks.

Jenna didn't want to show me pictures of the crash, but I forced her to. The image of this tree is burned in my memory now, with its gnarled branches and thick, twisted trunk. Hesitantly, I extend my hand and touch the rough bark.

My breath hitches, and a sob rakes through me. I lean

against the tree and try to stop the tears, but they just start flowing down my face. Hot, fat tears fall down my chin as I lean my head against the massive trunk.

I hear Martin's feet on the gravel and turn to see him on the side of the road. His face is impassable as he looks down at me. I know I look like a mess, but I can't stop the tears. I take a deep breath and look back toward the tree.

"I love you, Jack," I whisper to its branches. Wind rustles through the trees and more tears fall down my cheeks. I pull my jacket tighter and turn back toward Martin.

He's still standing by the side of the road. His face is completely blank, and he's staring at the tree. I wrap my arms around his waist, and it takes him a few seconds to hug me back.

"You okay?" I ask.

He takes a deep breath and looks at me as if he's seeing me for the first time. He nods. "Yeah. I should be asking you that, not the other way around."

I lean my cheek against his chest and take a deep breath.

"I haven't been back here since the accident."

"Me neither."

I frown, and then look up at him. He shakes his head. "I mean... I don't know. If I'd have known, I would have booked a place somewhere else..."

"No, it's okay," I say. I glance at the tree once more and take a deep breath. "It's good to come back here. It's..." I inhale sharply. "It's good to come back with you." I glance at Martin. "It doesn't feel like a coincidence, does it? It's like Jack wanted to meet you and make sure he approved."

Martin's face goes white, and he swallows thickly. I squeeze my arms around his waist. "I didn't mean to freak you out. Do you believe in ghosts?"

"I didn't."

"... but...?"

"I don't, I mean."

"Are you sure you're okay?"

"I'm fine." He untangles himself from my arms and turns his face away from me. "Just cold. You okay to keep driving?"

I frown and try to catch his eye, but he's already walking toward the car. It stings. Surely he would realize how significant this is for me?

Maybe it's just reminding him of Brianne, and he's not ready to face it. I glance back at the tree and take a deep breath. I say a silent goodbye to Jack and head back to the car.

When I get back in, Martin says nothing. His hands are gripping the steering wheel so tightly his knuckles are turning white. His jaw twitches as he puts his indicator on, and we drive off without wasting any time.

I stare at his profile and wonder if I should say anything. He doesn't look at me, or put his hand on my thigh, or say anything. He's just... there.

I didn't mean to hurt him or be awkward by stopping there. It just felt like the right time to say goodbye to Jack. To do it with Martin felt right, but maybe he's not at that point yet. His spouse died, too, and I need to remember that. Grief creeps up in unexpected ways.

I slide my hand over his thigh and he inhales. His shoulders relax slightly and he gives me a tight-lipped smile.

"Sorry."

"It's okay. I didn't mean to make you uncomfortable."

"You didn't." He opens his mouth as if he's going to keep talking, but he just puts his hand over mine and squeezes. He keeps his eyes on the road, and I turn to look out the windshield. I watch the forest go by and lean my head against the headrest.

A smile stretches over my lips. I finally feel at peace with

Jack's death. Stopping by the tree—touching it, and actually saying goodbye—it felt good. It feels like I'm honoring Jack's memory and allowing myself to move on.

I glance at Martin once more and I worry about him. I have to be patient, though. Grief comes in waves, and just because I'm starting to make peace with Jack's death doesn't mean he's there, too. We've found each other, and that's the important thing.

I turn on the radio and settle into my seat. Martin takes a deep breath, and the tension in his jaw eases.

It only takes forty-five more minutes for us to get to the cabin. My eyebrows arch when we drive up. It's a mansion nestled into the trees, with big windows under an A-line roof. We pull up and Martin turns off the car. He gets out without a word and stretches his arms up over his head. I walk around toward him and put my arm around his waist, but he pulls away.

I frown as he avoids my gaze. He grabs our bags from the trunk and heads for the front door without a word. I watch his broad back as he stalks toward the front door.

It stings.

It feels like right when I feel closer than I've ever felt to him, he's pulling away. He's hardly said two words since we stopped at the scene of my accident.

I watch him check his phone and then key in a code to a lock box. He pulls out a set of keys and opens the front door. He glances back at me, raising an eyebrow.

"You coming in?"

His eyes are hard, and there's no hint of a smile in his features. Lines on his forehead have appeared, and the color hasn't returned to his face yet. He looks like the Martin I met at the pool, back in January. Tortured and angry and bitter.

I swallow and nod.

"Yeah," I say. "I'm coming."

18

MARTIN

NICOLE KEEPS GLANCING AT ME, and I know she can tell that something is wrong. I unpack my bag in silence, and then head to the main room to start a fire. Maybe if I keep moving, I can give myself enough time to recover. If I just keep doing things, I won't have to face the truth.

I killed her husband.

I injured her—I broke her back!

I'm the reason she has medical bills, and I'm the reason the insurance company is stalling. It's a hit and run, and they don't have anyone to sue. They want to reject her claim and leave her in debt, in pain, grieving for her husband.

And it's because of me.

Me.

That car wasn't okay when I hit them. They didn't drive away. He *died*.

My heart starts palpitating and my hands tremble as I try to light a match. I snap the match in half and then take a deep breath.

I jump when Nicole's hands slide over my shoulders.

"Are you okay, Marty?"

"I'm fine!" The sound of my voice bounces off the high ceilings and echoes around us. Her eyes widen and she drops her hands off my shoulders. I take a deep breath, rubbing my temples.

"I'm sorry, babe," I say. "I just... when we stopped... I'm just sorry. About Jack. About you. About everything."

She takes a deep breath, chuckling softly. "Marty, it's not your fault. You have nothing to be sorry about."

My heart squeezes, and I can't breathe. If only she knew.

My God, what would happen if she knew? She'd never talk to me again! I'd never see her. I'd lose her, just like I lost Brianne.

I thought Brianne's death was the worst moment of my life, but I was wrong. What's worse than that is knowing that I am so close to having it all again—all the love, happiness, partnership—and it could all be snatched away from me. This, right now... this is the worst moment of my life.

I knew Nicole was too good to be true. I knew I didn't deserve her. I never should have let her in.

My hands shake as I try to light another match, and Nicole gently takes it from me. She lights the fire and I take a few moments to compose myself. I walk to the huge windows that give a perfect view of the mountains and lakes at our feet.

Maybe this is karma. It's not me getting a second chance at love. I scoff. A second chance? Me? No, this is punishment for my crime. This is God, or the Universe, or whatever other force there is showing me what a shitty fucking person I am. Tears prickle at my eyes and I fight to keep my composure.

Nicole appears by my side and hands me a beer.

"Fridge is stocked," she says. "This place is amazing."

I nod, taking a sip. She looks at me funny but says nothing. How will I get through this weekend?

Maybe I should just tell her. I could sit her down right now and tell her the truth. If I face this head-on, like a man, I can take responsibility for my actions. I can do what I was too fucked up to do last January.

But then, Nicole slides her arm around my waist and lays her head on my chest. Her hair smells so fucking good, and I know that I'm too weak.

I don't want to lose her. I can't let her go. If I tell her, she'll never forgive me. I won't be anything to her except the guy who killed her husband.

My heart starts to thump and Nicole looks at me again.

"Are you sure you're okay? Your heart is beating so fast. I can hear it."

I nod, taking another gulp of beer. "I'm good," I clear my throat. "We probably only have a few more hours of daylight. You want to go for a hike? There's some nice trails nearby."

"Fresh air would be good." She smiles at me, and her whole face beams. She's so fucking *good*. So kind and loving and generous. And I'm...

... I'm me. A killer. A coward.

I take a deep breath and kiss her temple. I try to smile at Nicole, but it feels like my face is creaking and cracking as my lips curl upward as if I've forgotten how to do it. I feel like I'm acting—faking it. I'm pretending to be someone I'm not.

Maybe that's all I've been doing for the past eighteen months.

Why didn't I just stop when I hit that car? Nicole told me herself that they sat there for half an hour without anyone driving by, and then they waited ten more minutes for the ambulance. I could have helped them! Instead, selfishly, I drove off.

I'm a *lawyer* for Christ's sake! I *knew* it was wrong, and I still did it.

I remember the tears running down my face, the adrenaline coursing through my veins, and the knowledge, deep in my heart, that I was too late for Brianne.

But still, I didn't stop for them. I let her husband die on the side of the road. I let her sit there with a broken back while I drove away like a monster.

Moving mechanically, I follow Nicole to the front door. I put my bottle of beer on the counter and slip my jacket on. She puts a hat on her head and smiles at me.

"Thank you for taking me here." She reaches over to squeeze my hand. Her touch is gentle, and I hate her for it.

I try to smile at her again. "It's my pleasure."

WHEN WE GET BACK, the sun is just touching the horizon. The sky is ablaze with colors, and Nicole's face is beaming. The beauty of the mountains disgusts me. I can't look at the sunset, or at Nicole, or at anything except the darkness in my soul.

I take a deep breath to steady myself. There are a couple of burger patties in the fridge, so I throw them on the barbeque. I overplay how tired I am whenever Nicole tries to make advances toward me. It feels wrong to be close to her, knowing what I know—knowing what I did.

After dinner, we sit on the couch together. She leans her head on my lap and I stroke her hair. I watch her eyes close as she falls asleep, and I trail my fingers down her arm and back up again.

Her breath is slow and steady, and emotion starts to build up inside me. I brush hot tears off my face, trying my best not to move her.

I don't want to wake her up. If I do, I'll have to explain

myself, and I don't want to lie. I'm already lying to her every minute that I don't tell her the truth.

She stirs awake, and I wipe my face.

"Let's go to bed." I brush the hair off her face. She smiles at me, and we head back toward the big king bed at the back of the cabin. When she strips down and gets under the covers, guilt pierces my heart again.

I shouldn't be allowed to be next to her perfect body, her perfect soul.

She presses her body next to mine, and the heat of her curves makes my body respond, even though I try to stop it. Her hand runs down my stomach and grips my cock. My breath hitches and I squeeze my eyes shut.

My body is betraying me. I shouldn't be hard right now. I shouldn't want this, but the ways she's moving and moaning next to me is making my head spin.

When she kneels down and puts her lips over my cock, I inhale. Fuck, it feels good. She takes my shaft in her mouth and I exhale, squeezing my eyes shut. With one hand on my shaft, and her mouth over my head, I feel like I'm going to explode. She moves faster and faster, knowing exactly what I like. She bobs up and down as the tension inside me builds.

I'm going to come. I don't want to. It's wrong.

If I wait any longer, I'm going to—

"Stop, stop," I say, pulling her off. "Stop. You're going to make me come."

"That's the point," she grins. Her hand slides down, gripping my cock again and I sigh.

I can't fight it. I can't deny it. I want her more than I've ever wanted anyone before. My heart thumps, and I shake my head.

"You're irresistible, Nicole."

The voice in my head that's screaming at me not to do it gets quieter as my desire for her grows. She bites her lip, reaching for my cock again. Darkness grips my heart and I let it take over. She looks into my eyes, and her lust makes me boil over.

I grip her by the waist and flip her over onto her back. Grabbing her arms, I pin them over her head. She yelps, and then stares at me with fire in her eyes.

"There you are," she says. "You're back. I was afraid you were gone."

"I'm right here," I growl, tightening my grip on her wrists. I spread her legs apart in one rough motion and she gasps, smiling. I growl again, rubbing my shaft along her wet slit. She sighs, closing her eyes and wriggling her body toward me.

"I want you." Her voice is soft, and I watch her perfect face relax as pleasure washes over her.

"I know you do." Back and forth, I rub my shaft along her slit. Her wetness drips out of her opening and coats me. My cock throbs.

"I'm on the pill."

My eyes widen, and the darkness inside me is all-consuming. We've never had sex without a condom. Nicole nods.

"Fuck me, Martin. I want to feel you. All of you."

It's wrong, but I don't care. My hand tightens around her wrists and I run my other hand down her side. I pinch her nipple, loving her little gasp. I run my hand between her legs and she moans.

Then, without waiting another second, I bury my cock inside her. From the tip to the hilt, I drive myself deep inside her. She gasps, rolling her hips toward me. She stretches to accept me, and I drag my cock out of her again.

"Is that what you want?" I growl in her ear, driving my cock deeper inside her. She screams. Her face is a mask of pleasure. I feel nothing except need. Need for her, need for release, need for my cock to be so deep inside her she forgets what day of the week it is.

"Answer me," I growl in her ear. My breath is hot on her shoulder and I punish her pussy again, fucking her harder and faster. "Is this what you want?"

"Yes," she pants. Her fingernails dig into my back, and the pain feels so fucking good. I thrust again and again until she comes all over my cock, quivering and trembling and screaming my name.

I hook my arms on her shoulders as her walls clamp down around my cock. *Fuck*, she feels so good. This is wrong, but my body is out of my control. She's arching and scratching and screaming and I just fuck her again and again and again. I throw her legs onto my shoulders and bury my pain deep inside her pussy.

I don't deserve her, and I don't care. I'm taking her.

With that thought gnawing at my heart, I fuck her harder than ever before, and I fill her sweet little pussy with my seed until it dribbles out of her.

Mine.

The thought crosses my mind without warning. I watch my orgasm drip out of her swollen, red lips, and then I lay down beside her. She interlaces her fingers in mine and lets out a sigh.

"That was incredible."

I close my eyes and grunt in response.

19

NICOLE

SOMETHING IS OFF. At first, I think it's only in my head. As the weekend goes on, though, I know I'm not imagining it. Martin is distant. Most of the time, he won't even look me in the eye. By the time Sunday afternoon comes around, it feels like we're both looking forward to the weekend being over.

He only really looks at me when we have sex. And my goodness... the sex. It's unlike anything I've ever experienced. It's angry and intense and it makes me come harder than ever before. My whole body is sore, swollen, raw, and thoroughly exhausted.

But it's *good*. We bite and claw at each other, as if we're unleashing something from the deep, dark recesses of our hearts. When we finish, we don't speak. Usually, Martin rolls away from me and I go to the bathroom to clean up.

I've never had so many intense orgasms, and I don't know how I feel about it. I'm almost embarrassed at how turned on I get when he looks at me with that pain in his eyes. When he comes, his whole body shudders and I relish the feeling of him emptying himself inside me. I want his pain. I want his hurt. I want everything he has to give me.

Something has changed.

We drive back in relative silence. When we pass the site of my car accident, I say nothing. I try to act casual, because I think that's what set this whole thing off. When we stopped here on the way to the cabin, that's when things shifted between us.

I give him a kiss goodbye when he drops me off at my apartment. I don't invite him in, and he doesn't ask to come up. When I get inside, I take a deep breath and pull out my phone. I stare at the blank screen for a few seconds, and then I look around my apartment.

It feels cold and lonely. I think about my weekend—about our sex. My mind starts to spiral and I know I can't be alone. I call my sister Jenna, but she doesn't pick up.

Hesitating, I scroll through my phone and dial my friend Stella. I haven't put any effort into friendships for the past few months. Before I got a job, it was too depressing to see other people happy. After I got the job, I guess I got caught up with Martin.

But now, I feel very much alone.

"Nic!" Stella exclaims as she picks up the phone. "I haven't heard from you in forever!"

"I know, I'm sorry."

"Don't apologize. I've been all over the place. Did I tell you I bought a house?"

"Yeah, you did. A few months ago, right?"

"Yes, well, it's been an absolute nightmare. The inspection missed so many things, and I had to get the roof patched in the middle of winter. Then, I found out there were structural problems in the basement, and—gosh, I'm babbling. I'm sorry. How are you? Are you free? You want to meet up for a glass of wine? I'm so sick of staring at this house. It just stresses me out."

I lean against the back of my couch and relief spreads through me. I shouldn't have let so many friendships fall away.

"That sounds great, actually. You want to go to The Blue Room?"

"I'll meet you there in twenty."

WHEN SHE WALKS into the bar, I've already sat down and ordered us two glasses of Pinot Grigio. She spreads her arms and hugs me so hard I wince.

"Oh, geez," she says. "Sorry. Is your back still sore?"

"Not so much anymore, swimming helps."

"And it helps the figure as well," she says, wiggling her eyebrows. "You are looking fantastic. You're glowing!"

I laugh, shaking my head. Our wine arrives, and I ask Stella about her house. She tells me about nightmare renovations, pipes bursting, leaky roofs. She's got bags under her eyes, and she finishes her wine in four big gulps.

She picks up her empty glass. "This is empty!"

I laugh. "Yep."

"I must be drinking faster than I thought. It's that darn house."

"Well, at least you have the cash to buy a house," I grin.

"How are you? Did Jack's insurance come through?"

I shake my head. "Still waiting. I think they're delaying because it was a hit and run. They've been asking me all kinds of questions. Either that or they're trying to say it was related to skiing, which isn't covered since it's a 'high risk activity', or whatever."

"It was a car accident!" She shakes her head and motions to the bartender for more wine. "Insurance companies are scumbags."

I sigh, and Stella glances at me.

"Something else is up."

I laugh, shaking my head. "It's nothing."

"You call me, out of the blue, on a Sunday night. I don't think you did that to hear me complaining about my new house."

"You're right," I grin. "I, uh... I've gotten myself into a situation."

Her eyebrow arches. I've known Stella for about seven years—we used to be paralegals together. She left to go to law school and is now a full-fledged lawyer. Her eyes have always been sharp, but now it seems like she misses nothing.

"What kind of situation?"

I clear my throat. "I may have slept with a coworker."

Her lips twitch. "I'm listening."

"Well, he's more of a boss, really. Not directly, but he could be."

"A partner at the firm?"

I nod.

"Oh, Nicole," she sighs.

"No, everything was great! He... he lost his wife last year, too. We..." I sigh. Our wine arrives and I take a big sip. "We get along really well. I mean *really* well."

"And the sex is good?"

"Very good."

"So what's the problem?"

"Well," I start. I take a deep breath. The words just don't seem to want to come out. Finally, with Stella still watching me, I explain. "He took me on this weekend getaway to the mountains—to this gorgeous log cabin."

"Very romantic."

"It was! Except on the way there, we passed the site of the accident."

"Oh gosh."

"I asked to stop. It felt... significant. I went to the spot where we hit the tree, and it felt like Jack's presence was there. I just... it was *nice*. And it was nice to be there with Martin. It felt like I was ready to move on from it all, insurance money or not."

Stella nods and tilts her head. "So what's the problem?"

"Well, Martin kind of... *changed*."

"What do you mean?"

"He's not himself. He barely looked at me after that, barely touched me. The sex was... I don't know, *angry*. Or just intense, I guess. It was *good*, don't get me wrong. But..." I shake my head. "I don't know."

"Maybe it all reminded him of his wife. You said he lost his spouse?"

"That's what I thought. But anytime I tried to ask him anything he just shut down."

"He probably just needs more time. Not everyone grieves the same way."

I nod. Now it's my turn to look at my near-empty wine glass in surprise. Stella laughs.

"I think there's a hole in our glasses, because there's no way we're drinking this quickly."

I smile. I need to change the subject. Worry is starting to weigh me down, so I turn to Stella. "How's work, anyway?"

"It's good. Busy—I'm sure you're the same. It seems like it never stops."

We move on from the conversation, and the burden on my shoulders seems a little bit lighter. When we finish our third glass of wine, we both stand up and waver.

"That wine went straight to my head." Stella grabs onto the back of a chair to steady herself.

"Just like the old days."

We lean on each other and walk out. We share a taxi, since my place is on the way to hers. Before I get out, I wrap my arms around her and squeeze her tight.

"It was really good to see you."

"You too." Her voice is muffled in my coat. "We need to hang out more often."

"Maybe I can help you with the house renovations."

"Be careful," she laughs. "I might just take you up on that."

"I'm pretty good with a hammer."

"That's terrifying."

I laugh and bid her goodbye. This time, when I get inside, I let out a deep breath. I'm a little tipsy, but that's not why I feel better. I think I've gotten too caught up in the whirlwind with Martin. I need to take a step back, to think about what is best for me.

It feels like I've moved on from Jack, but that doesn't mean I need to go all-in with Martin. He's got just as much baggage as I do, and how can we support each other if we're both struggling?

I get ready for bed, checking my phone one last time before snuggling into the covers. There's no message from Martin, and as much as I try to tell myself I don't care, I know that I'm disappointed.

20

MARTIN

THIS TIME, when I wake up for work, I'm not excited. I'm dreading it. I drag my feet out of bed and stand under the shower, unmoving. I open my mouth and drink a bit of shower water, and then finally start washing myself. By the time I've made myself a coffee and had some breakfast, I'm leaving for work a full half hour later than usual.

I avoid Nicole's desk on the way in, but I can't avoid Carmen's. She calls out to me when I walk past her office.

"Martin, so good of you to show up today!"

I poke my head in and see her with one of our biggest clients. Julian is a chart-topping musician, and in his ripped jeans and casual tee-shirt, he looks very out of place in Carmen's sleek, modern office.

"Julian," I say, extending my hand. "Good to see you."

"Not sure I can say the same," he grimaces. "I'd rather not be in here at all."

Carmen gives me a look, and gestures to a chair. I take a seat beside Julian, and Carmen explains.

"Julian has gotten himself in a bit of trouble. It shouldn't be too hard to fight—it's a DUI."

"Who's the judge?"

"Judge Harkin."

"Fuck," I say under my breath.

Julian shakes his head. "This guy has it out for me. I didn't even do anything to him!"

"He has it out for everyone who he thinks could be a bad influence on the 'youths', as he calls them," I explain. "Since you're in the public eye, and your audience includes lots of young people, I would expect he wants to make an example out of you."

"He said exactly that," Carmen answers. "Martin, I'd like you to take the case."

I nod. "No problem." Carmen glances at Julian and then back at me. I frown. "Anything I should know?"

Julian sighs. His chin falls to his chest and he runs his fingers through his hair. "I hit someone."

The wind gets knocked out of me. No. I can't take this. I can't have anything to do with this. No, no, no. Nicole would never forgive me. I can't do that to her.

But I sit there, and don't say anything. What possible reason could I give to refuse this case? Julian is one of our most famous and *richest* clients. He pays us a huge retainer to deal with these exact types of situations.

So I just clear my throat. "And this person you hit... are they alive?"

"Yes!" Julian says, whipping his head toward me. "Fuck man, I'm not a killer!"

A knife goes straight through my heart, and I do my best to keep my face blank. "Of course."

Carmen interjects. "The woman he hit is in the hospital. Her injuries are relatively minor, but her husband is pushing her to press charges."

"I see."

"So can you help me out?" Julian stares at me, his eyebrows arched. I can see a hint of desperation in his eyes.

I nod. "Yes."

Julian blows the air out of his mouth and nods. "Alright."

"Until then," Carmen says, "you do as the judge says and you do not drive. Not even once. Not in a deserted parking lot. Not out on country roads. You don't have a license, and if you're caught again, you will go to jail."

Julian grins. "Got it."

"This is serious."

"I know."

By the time I leave Carmen's office, my head is spinning. I know that I have to take Julian's case. He's a huge client for the firm, and Carmen asked me specifically. That's not the kind of thing I can refuse. Plus, it's not like I can explain why I don't want to work on the case.

Judge Harkin is tough, but I think we can settle this with no jail time, and hopefully not much press. Carmen is an expert at making these kinds of things go away, and I expect she'll be pulling as many strings as possible. Maybe Nicole doesn't even have to find out. I could try to keep her out of it.

It doesn't feel right. That's just lying to her... again.

I slump down on my office chair and stare at my blank computer screen. I sigh, and finally turn on my computer. Might as well get to work.

It's almost eleven in the morning when my office door flies open. I hear my assistant Kelly protesting, but Nicole comes storming through the door anyways.

"A DUI case? With a woman in the hospital?"

I stare at her without speaking. My cock throbs under my desk at the sight of her, marching in here guns blazing. It's wrong, but her anger is so fucking hot. Her dark hair is falling out of her bun, and her cheeks have a spot of red on them.

But it's her eyes that are striking. They're blazing, burning through me as she leans her knuckles on my desk. I'd love to bend her over this desk and fuck the anger right out of her.

"You don't have anything to say for yourself?" Her voice is calm, steady, but it has an undercurrent of tension. I hold her gaze for a few moments and then shrug.

"I didn't have a choice."

"You *always* have a choice, Martin!"

"That's not how life works."

"What the fuck is that supposed to mean?"

"This is my *job*, Nicole."

"Yes, and you've been fucking me for weeks, making me feel like I mean something to you. I just showed you where my husband *died*, for Christ's sake! Probably exactly like this poor woman—hit by a drunkard on her way home."

"You weren't hit by a drunk driver."

She frowns. "How the fuck would you know?"

"I... there's no evidence," I stammer. I sigh, waving her away. "Look, Carmen gave me the case. Julian is one of the firm's biggest clients."

Her face crumples and she shakes her head. She opens her mouth, but just keeps shaking her head. When she finally does speak, her voice is nothing more than a strained whisper.

"Why are you doing this?"

My heart hardens and my blood turns to ice. All the places where Nicole has softened me start to harden again. I shake my head.

"I have to do my job."

"You've always chosen your cases. What about the medical misconduct case?"

"Nicole, grow up!" I explode. "These cases—Julian's DUI—these are the cases that *allow* me to take on the ones that actually make a difference. This is about more than justice. It's about money."

She snorts, nodding her head. "It's always about money, isn't it? That's what it all comes down to, in the end."

She stares at me for a long moment, and then turns around and walks out. Kelly is standing just outside the door, wide-eyed. I wave to the door.

"Close that fucking door, will you?"

She nods without a word and closes me into my office. I exhale loudly, dropping my forehead into my hands. I've fucked up.

Who am I kidding? Taking the case isn't fucking up. Doing a hit and run was a fuck up! Lying to Nicole by not telling her right away was a fuck up!

Now what am I supposed to do? If I come clean, I'll lose everything. I'll lose my job—I won't be the youngest partner at the firm anymore, I'll be the youngest partner to ever get fired. I'll lose my reputation. I might even get disbarred.

I'll lose Nicole.

What difference would that make? I'm pretty sure I've already lost her.

21

NICOLE

I'M FUMING when I sit back down at my desk. Clarissa, the other paralegal, slides her chair over toward me.

"You okay?"

"No."

She puts her hand on my shoulder. "Want to go out for a coffee and a talk?"

I look at her and take a deep, shuddering breath. "No, thanks Clarissa. I... I don't know what I need right now."

She nods. "Okay, well, let me know."

I turn back to my computer to try to hide the tears in my eyes. She gets the hint and backs away toward her desk. I sniffle, wiping my eyes. The screen blurs, and I take a deep breath. This is torture. I head for the bathrooms and lock the door. Then, I splash water on my face and take deep, gulping breaths.

Staring at myself in the mirror for a few seconds, I prepare myself for what I'm about to do. A thousand thoughts fly around my head.

I need this job—it's the only reason I can still afford

physio. I'm pain-free most days now, and if I give up the job, I might have to give up physio, too.

I won't be able to make payments on my bills. I'll struggle to make rent again. I'll go back to how life was before, when I was in a deep, dark hole with no way out.

Taking a deep breath, I square my shoulders. I can find a new job. I turn away from the mirror and lean against the counter. I stare at the tiles on the floor, my eyes travelling up and down the lines of grout.

If I get angry about Martin taking this case but I keep working here, then I'm a hypocrite.

There's no other choice.

I have to quit.

I can't reasonably keep working here, when I'll be working for the people who defend the scumbag that killed Jack. Well, not the exact scumbag, but it might as well be the same thing. People shouldn't be able to get away with these things.

A woman is in hospital, and my husband is dead. All because of people like Julian, who thinks he's above the law.

My hands shake as I pull out my phone. I dial Jenna and breathe a sigh of relief when she answers.

"Jenna, I think I need to quit."

She's silent for a beat, and then takes a deep breath. "Okay. Are you sure?"

"One of their famous clients—Julian, the singer. You know him?"

"Doesn't he sing 'If You Want Me'? I didn't know he was your client"

"Yeah, that one. He hit a woman in a DUI. They're going to defend him and try to get the charges dropped. I just..." My voice cracks. "I can't be a part of that."

"Oh, Nicole," Jenna sighs. "I'm so sorry."

"I just keep thinking about Jack, you know? I drove by the place where he died on Saturday, and I don't know, maybe it's just all fresh in my mind. But this Julian prick could have killed the woman! He could have done exactly what happened to me. And he could get *away* with it! Just like the guy who killed Jack got away with it."

"Oh, Nicole," Jenna says again. "Oh, babe."

I sniffle, covering my eyes with my hand.

Jenna sighs. "But Nic, if you quit, it doesn't stop them from defending him. It'll only hurt you."

"I know."

"This job has been the best thing that's happened to you in a year."

"I'm not so sure about that anymore."

"What are you going to do after? Would you find another job? It's not like law firms aren't going to take questionable cases."

I sigh. "I know, I know. It's just... Jenna, I've been seeing one of the partners. Dating. Or... sleeping with him. I don't know what it's been."

"Oh, gosh."

"Yeah. And I told him about Jack. I showed him the spot where he died, and he *still* took the case! How am I supposed to work alongside him now? I just..." I sob.

Jenna sighs over the phone. "Just do what you have to do, Nicole. I'll always be here for you."

I sniffle, nodding. "Yeah. Thanks, Jen."

"I'm not asking you right now, because I'm aware of how upset you are, but I'm expecting more details later."

I snort-laugh and shake my head. "I don't want to talk about it. It's too embarrassing. God, I was so stupid! I actually thought that he cared about me. He reminded me of Jack, and..."

"Don't beat yourself up about it, Nicole."

"Easier said than done."

"I hope you gave him shit for taking the case."

"I marched into his office and yelled at him. I was so close to slapping him across the face."

"Good. Take the rest of the day off and come over here. I'll make you some chocolate chip cookies."

"You're such a mom," I say, shaking my head. "You used to hate baking."

"Well, having two kids does, in fact, turn you into a mom."

I chew my lip and sigh. "Cookies sound nice."

"Come on. I hate hearing you like this. Just leave that horrible place and come here. We can write your letter of resignation together, and then you can give it to your boss tomorrow. Everything will work out."

"That sounds good."

We hang up the phone and I take a deep breath. Jenna is right. I just need to get out of here today, and then I can sort my head out. I glance at myself in the mirror and smooth my hair, and then I take a deep breath. I walk back to my desk and nod to Clarissa.

"I'm taking the afternoon off."

Her eyebrows lift up. "Yeah?"

I nod. "Not feeling well. I'll see you tomorrow."

"See you tomorrow." She smiles at me and gives me a small nod. It almost feels like she's saying *good for you*. I gather my things and walk out of the office with my head held high.

When I get to Jenna's house, she already has a batch of chocolate chip cookies in the oven, and water boiled for tea. I sit down on one of her creaky kitchen chairs and she puts a steaming mug of tea in front of me. She pours one for herself and takes a deep breath, shaking her head as she looks at me.

"You sure do know how to get yourself into trouble."

I grin. "Those cookies smell good."

"Don't change the subject," she laughs. "Even when you and Jack started dating. Do you remember how angry Dad was when you moved in together?"

"He didn't speak to me for five months," I laugh. "But he got over it."

"I think he met Jack properly and figured out he was the best thing for you."

My chest tightens and I nod. "He kept me grounded. I wasn't so impulsive when he was around."

Jenna takes a deep breath and smiles at me. "I don't know, I think it's good to see a bit of the old you again."

"What do you mean?"

"You were still impulsive and a bit reckless with Jack. But then, when he died, that all went away. You were so... empty. It's like you lost your personality." Her eyes mist up, and she shakes her head. "I thought I'd lost you."

A lump forms in my throat, and then Jenna laughs through her tears.

"But now, I mean, sleeping with a coworker and causing a scene at the office... that's the Nicole I know and love. That's my shit-head little sister."

We laugh until the buzzer on the oven goes off, and then we eat warm chocolate chip cookies and talk and talk until her kids come home from school.

This time, I stay over for dinner. The pain I used to feel being around her happy family is gone. This is my family, and they've always been here for me.

22

MARTIN

After an hour or so, I work up the courage to walk over to Nicole's desk. I need to make her understand that I get how she's feeling, but I have no choice.

You always have a choice, she said.

It's easy to say that, but how much choice do I really have? Maybe if I just explain that this is my job—she should know that already! She's worked in law long enough.

I take a deep breath and turn the corner, but I frown when I see her desk empty. Her computer is off, too, which means...

"Is Nicole gone?"

Clarissa glances at me and nods. Her stare is cold. "Yep."

"Is she coming back?"

"She wasn't feeling well, so no, I don't think so."

"She was fine this morning."

Clarissa's eyebrow rises in a slow arch, and she stares at me for a few seconds. I try not to squirm where I stand, and anger flares up inside me.

"Fine. If she comes back, can you tell her I want to talk to her?"

"Mmm," Clarissa says, turning back to her screen. "I'll get right on that."

I stare at the paralegal, slack-jawed. Three months ago, she would have been afraid to talk to me. She would have jumped when I told her to.

Now?

She's been spending too much fucking time with Nicole.

I stomp out of the office and head downstairs. I need some air. As soon as the fresh air hits my face, I take a deep breath. The sun is shining and a warm breeze washes over me, and I hate the weather for being nice. Pulling out my phone, I dial Nicole's number.

It goes straight to voicemail—she's turned her phone off. I groan, staring up at the sky above me. The clouds passing by start to make me nauseous when Carmen's voice appears by my ear.

"Looking for a defense to bring to Judge Harkin?" She asks. "Don't know if you'll find it up there." I look at her and snort, shaking my head.

"Just needed some air."

"What from?"

I sigh, shaking my head. "Nothing."

"Wouldn't be from our young, sassy, smart-mouthed paralegal, would it?"

I take a deep breath. There's no point denying it, everyone knows that Nicole and I have been involved. We haven't exactly been discreet about it.

"Didn't anybody ever tell you not to shit where you eat?"

I glance at Carmen and snort. "What about that intern you were always working late with last year?"

"Fuck off, Marty," she grins. She looks at me, putting her hand on my shoulder. It's weird to have actual physical contact with her.

"You're just doing your job, Martin," she says. "Your job is to defend that little shit, Julian, to the best of your abilities. That's why you get a paycheck. That's why your parking spot is right next to the door. That's why you can afford that fancy house you live in."

"I know, Carmen."

"So start acting like it."

I sigh and I stare at the clouds. Why did it have to be *now*, though? With that exact case? Right after I found out what I've done to Nicole?

"I never thought you were so sentimental," Carmen says. She grins at me, shaking her head. "You're smitten."

"I'm not a teenage girl with a crush on a boy band."

"No, you're a grown man who's smitten with his employee."

"She's not *my* employee."

"Another astute observation, Henderson. She's not your employee. She's *my* employee. And so are you."

I glance at her, nodding. "Yeah, yeah. I get it."

"I don't think you do." She squares her shoulders, looking me dead in the eye. Her eyes darken and I resist the urge to take a step back.

"Carmen, I get it," I say. My voice sounds stronger than I feel, and that pisses me off. I'm sick of feeling like this. Ever since Nicole walked into my life, everything has been off-balance. I can't think straight, I can't do my job.

"Martin, you need to do your fucking job," she says, her voice steady and cold. "I made you a partner at this firm. Don't let that be a mistake."

She stares at me for a few moments and I sigh as she walks away. Her back is straight as an arrow, and she has her chin held high. Her hips sway with a purposeful, powerful movement with every stride. I stare after her as my face twists and the taste in my mouth turns to ash.

I want to kick something, or punch something. I look at the cars parked in front of me and I wish I had the strength to flip them over. I'd take a baseball bat and smash every single fucking window.

Instead, I just stand there, fuming. I curl my fists into balls as the steam blows out of my ears and nose.

Yes, it's my job. Yes, I'm going to do it. That doesn't change the fact that I betrayed Nicole. I feel the walls around my heart start to build, brick by brick, until the warmth that Nicole brought into my life is all but snuffed out.

No, Carmen is right. I can't get sentimental. I can't get distracted. If Nicole doesn't like it, she can leave. I've made it this far without her—I made partner, I climbed the ladder, I became one of the most successful lawyers in Colorado.

And I'm going to fuck that up for a *woman*? I'm going to throw that all away because the light in Nicole's eyes reminds me of my dead wife?

Get a fucking grip, Martin. Pull yourself together and remember what's important here.

Me. That's what's important. My career. My life. My salary.

I'll lose it all if I tell Nicole the truth. I'll lose it all if I don't take the case.

If I don't just *Do. My. Job.*

My heart hardens as I take a deep breath. I glance up and down the road at the people walking by, oblivious to the torture going on in my mind.

Turning back toward the office, my mind is made up.

I choose my life. I choose my career. I choose Julian's case.

As I'm sucked through the building's revolving door, a

part of me stays outside, watching myself walk away. Another piece of my doomed heart dies, and I'm glad for it.

23

NICOLE

I PAT my purse with my hand, knowing that my letter of resignation is sitting in there like an atomic bomb. I'm giving up my salary, my health insurance... and Martin.

But is it really giving him up if I never had him to begin with? Maybe he was just using me. I wasn't special, or different. I was convenient.

Cracks spider over my heart and I take a deep breath. When I walk into the firm, I head straight for Carmen's office. She's already here, as usual. She's always here. The woman works like no one I've ever met before. She's strong and powerful and I respect her, but I just can't work for her anymore.

I pause before going in, taking a deep breath to steel myself. I remember Jenna's calming words last night as she helped me compose my letter.

"Do it for Jack, Nic," she'd said. "Be true to yourself and honor his memory."

I take a deep breath and knock on Carmen's door.

"Come in," she says. When I push the door open, she doesn't look up. She's scratching something down on her huge stack of papers, her reading glasses perched on the end of her nose.

I clear my throat. She looks up, sliding the glasses off her face and arching her eyebrows in surprise.

"Nicole."

"Carmen, hi." I clear my throat again, shifting awkwardly from foot to foot. She gestures to one of the chairs across her desk. I sit down, holding my purse over my thighs. I take a deep breath, and Carmen folds her hands on her desk. Her gaze is unflinching, and she just waits for me to start.

"First of all, I wanted to thank you for everything you've done for me. Working here has been a great opportunity, and I've learned so much."

Start with something nice to soften the blow.

Carmen leans back in her chair, still pointing those laser beam eyes at me.

I take a deep breath and reach into my purse. "I'd like to hand in my resignation. I've put my last day as two weeks from today. I want you to know that it's nothing personal, I've just decided that I need to focus on healing from the accident."

I slide the letter across the desk and Carmen looks at it for a brief moment. She tents her hands in front of her, tapping the pads of her fingers against each other.

"What brought this on, Nicole?"

She doesn't make a move to touch the letter.

I take a deep breath. Does she know about me and Martin? Probably. There have been enough whispers around the office, she'd have to be seriously out of touch not to know.

"It's not because of Martin, is it? That would be a real shame."

So she does know.

I shrug and shake my head. I'm not really sure how to answer.

Carmen takes a deep breath. "It would be a shame to lose such a valuable employee because of a... *personal* matter."

She thinks I'm a valuable employee? I stare at a spot on her desk and try to gather my thoughts. I didn't think this would be so difficult. I thought I was sure, but now, with Carmen's eyes stripping me bare, I'm not so sure.

The door opens behind us.

"I think I found a way to get Julian's case thrown out," Martin's deep, husky voice starts. He stops when he sees me, his mouth hanging open. He glances at my face, and then Carmen's. "I'll come back."

He doesn't look at me again before turning around and walking out of her office, and I know it's over. If I didn't know it before, I know it now. He chose the case. He chose himself. He chose to disregard everything I've told him about my husband and my accident.

He's never cared about me.

I straighten my back and turn toward Carmen, sliding the letter of resignation toward her with my fingers.

"Thank you for everything."

She sighs, reaching for the letter. She doesn't open the envelope, she just taps it on her desk. She lays it aside and goes back to the stack of files beside her. She doesn't look up when she speaks.

"I'll call security. You can empty your desk and they'll escort you out."

My eyebrows shoot up. "I thought... two weeks... I didn't..."

"You'll get two weeks' pay from today. We have lots of confidential, sensitive case information. When someone quits or is fired, they need to be off the premises the same day. It's protocol."

"Protocol, right," I stammer. I clear my throat. "Well, alright."

Carmen looks up at me and I try to straighten my face. My eyes are misting, and I hate myself for it. I try to keep my chin up and hold her gaze. I bite my lip to keep it from trembling.

I hate how weak I feel. I hate how I'm second-guessing myself, how I'm not sure, how I've let Martin worm his way into my life and ruin everything for me.

Yet, here I am. Trying to stop myself from spilling tears in my boss's office right after quitting. Carmen takes a deep breath, pushing herself up to stand. She extends a hand toward me. I take a tentative step toward her, and then shake her hand.

Her handshake is firm, strong, unwavering. She looks me in the eye and dips her chin down.

"If you need a recommendation, let me know. You are very good at your job."

"Thanks, Carmen," I say. She nods, and then looks back at her work. I let myself out, closing the door softly behind me.

By the time I get to my desk, there's a security guard waiting for me. I nod to him. I take my favorite pen, and a picture of me, Jenna, and her family. I open my drawers and see bits and pieces of stationary, closing them back up one by one.

In the bottom drawer, I pull out my workout bag with my swim cap and bathing suit. I sling it over my shoulder and then nod to the security guard.

"All set?"

"All set," I answer.

Clarissa comes around the corner with a coffee cup in her hand and her eyes widen.

"What's...?"

"I handed in my resignation," I explain. "This is protocol, apparently," I motion to the security guard. He grunts.

Clarissa sets her mug down and puts her hands on her hips. She sighs, shaking her head.

"I was just starting to enjoy having you around," she says, smiling. "What happened?"

"Personal differences, I guess."

"Is this because of that bastard, Martin?"

I snort, shaking my head. "I don't even know anymore. Take care of yourself."

She wraps me in a hug, squeezing me close. With her arms around me, I feel like I've made the right decision. She nods to me.

"Good luck."

I walk out with the security guard. I don't stop him when he walks in the direction of Martin's office. I don't turn my head, and my steps don't falter. I just keep walking, even though I can feel everyone's eyes on me.

The security guard escorts me to my car, and then I nod to him.

"I'll take it from here," I say sarcastically. "You've been quite the gentleman." His furry eyebrows draw together in confusion and I shake my head. "Never mind."

I get in my car and take a deep breath. When I exit the building, it simultaneously feels like a weight is lifted off my shoulders, and like my heart is being ground to a fine dust.

I don't know whether to laugh or throw up.

Instead, I just head to the pool and try to swim my misery away.

24

MARTIN

SHE DOESN'T LOOK at me when she walks by my office. I watch her walk by through the open doorway. Without realizing what I'm doing, I get up and stand in my doorway. I watch her walk proudly toward the elevators, with the oaf of a security guard standing next to her.

He puts his hand on her mid back as they step into the elevator and a flash of jealousy courses through me. I want to rip his head clean off his neck for touching her perfect body. The elevator doors close and she's gone, and my stomach turns. I feel sick.

This is my fault.

When the shock wears off, the agony sets in. My chest aches as I curl my fists into my hair. I double over at the waist, squeezing my eyes shut.

When I straighten myself up again, agony is replaced with anger. It starts in my heart and spreads like venom through my veins. Soon, my anger carries me toward Carmen's office.

I rip the door open, letting it bang against the wall as I step through. It swings back behind me and I march toward her desk.

"You fucking *fired* her? What did she do to you?" I lean over her desk. Carmen removes her glasses and stares at me placidly.

"Answer me!" My voice is strained. My vocal cords feel like they've been rubbed with sandpaper. My pulse is quick and my blood feels hot and thick. Anger clouds my vision and Carmen's silence only intensifies it.

She stares at me for a few more moments. When she speaks, her voice is calm.

"You're out of line, Henderson."

"Fuck you!"

"You're out of line!" She shouts. My chest heaves as we stare at each other, and I try to register the shock of her yelling. I let out a sigh and kick one of her chairs, wincing as pain explodes through my toe.

"This fucking DUI case! We shouldn't even be defending that little shit bag!"

"That little shit bag pays for your mortgage, Martin," she replies icily. My breath rakes through my body, rattling my bones with every inhalation. I curl and uncurl my fists, staring at a blank place on the wall.

"If you must know, not that I need to explain myself to you, *ever*," Carmen says coolly, "Nicole quit."

I whip my head toward her, frowning.

"What?"

She lifts up a sealed envelope and waves it at me.

"Seems to me like I should be asking *you* what the fucking problem is," she says. She puts the letter down on her desk and I stare at it numbly.

She quit.

She's gone.

It's over.

If it wasn't clear before, it's crystal clear now. Nicole

doesn't want anything to do with me. She'll put herself in financial hardship just to stay away from me.

Pain pierces through me and I take a deep breath. I stand up taller.

Good riddance. She was a distraction anyway. She got under my skin, and she didn't deserve my attention. She was just a fucking paralegal. A fling.

I nod to Carmen, stalking out without a word. I walk back to my office, but I can't face working right now. Instead, I turn toward the elevators and I make my way to my car. My feet carry me without me knowing where I'm headed. The anger blazes through me, mingling with the strange, unfamiliar pain throbbing through my heart.

Putting the car in gear, I race out of the lot. I let my instincts take me through the streets, drumming my fingers on the steering wheel when a red light dares to stop me. Gritting my teeth, I press on the accelerator as soon as it turns green.

Before I know it, I'm outside Nicole's apartment. There's no time to analyze what's going on. No time to think about what I'm doing, or why I'm here. I mash on the buzzer over and over, but there's no response. An old woman shuffles out of the door, giving me a suspicious glare.

"I'm one of Nicole's friends," I say, forcing a smile. She frowns at me but lets me pass. I take the stairs two by two, heading for her door. I bang on her apartment, yelling her name. I listen, but all I can hear is my own ragged breath and the pounding of my heartbeat in my ears.

I lean my forehead against the door, sighing.

"Nicole," I say once more to the impassive door.

"What are you doing here?" I jump when I hear her voice behind me. Her hair is wet, and her eyes are rimmed with the red imprint from her swimming goggles. She has a towel slung over her arm, with her work bag hanging off her shoulder.

Her eyes are dark—almost black. They're so far from the sparkling grey that I've learned to love. She stares at me until I speak.

"Why did you quit?"

"Why did you take the DUI case?"

"Nicole..."

"Can you please move out of the way?"

I take a step aside as the anger flares inside me. Why won't she just *listen*? Why can't she just understand that this is my job, and I have to take whatever case Carmen gives me? I'm not doing this just to spite her. She shouldn't have quit.

She walks into her apartment leaving the door open, and I take that as an invitation inside. I step inside, closing the door behind me. She glances over her shoulder and takes a deep breath. Tossing her bag and towel over the back of a chair, she rakes her fingers through her wet hair and turns toward me.

Nicole plants her hands on her hips, facing me with all the force of her righteous anger.

"Why are you here?"

"Don't quit." It's not a request. She shouldn't be quitting over something so trivial. Bullshit cases go through the firm all the time, and it's our job to take them. She should know that by now. Why would she quit over *this*?

"That isn't your decision." Her defiance makes my blood boil. Lust ignites in my core and my cock hardens to steel in an instant. Her eyes flash at me, and I'd like nothing more than to teach her swollen lips a lesson.

I take a step toward her, and she stands her ground.

"Nicole."

Her chin juts upward. She sets her jaw, staring me straight in the eye. Why does she have to be so damn irresistible?

"I don't want you to quit," I say quietly, taking another step toward her. There's only a foot of space between us, and I close it with another step. She hasn't moved. Her chest brushes against mine, and my whole body zips with heat when I feel her nipples harden against me.

Her body leans into me and she forces herself backward, turning her face away from me.

"It doesn't matter what *you* want, Martin," she says. "It's done now."

"This isn't done."

"It's not your decision."

She takes a step away from me, but I catch her wrist with my hand. I pull her to me, sliding my other hand to the back of her neck and tilting her head up. I crush my lips against hers and kiss her more fiercely than ever before. Her mouth opens, inviting me in. She moans softly into my mouth as I let my tongue dance over hers, and then I kiss her harder. Our lips, tongues, teeth crash together as my hand on her neck tightens and her fist curls into my chest.

She smells like chlorine, and she tastes sweeter than honey. I groan, grinding my hard cock against her stomach as I pull her closer.

Then, as suddenly as it started, she pushes me back. Before I know what's happening, she lifts her arm and brings her hand across my face—*hard*.

"How *dare* you?"

Her eyes are blazing, her whole body trembling. I bring my hand up to my cheek in shock, arching my eyebrows.

"Don't pretend you didn't want that, princess."

"Get. Out." Her voice is low. I don't move, and her body vibrates. "*Out!*"

Her yell pierces straight through the center of my chest, and I take a step back. Lust and anger and guilt and rage boil inside me until I just turn around and rip the door open. I stand in the open doorway with my back to her for a moment, and finally turn my head to look over my shoulder.

"I thought you were different."

"Fuck you, Martin."

I leave the door open as I walk out the door and out of her life.

25

NICOLE

I'M STILL SHAKING when I pick up the phone and call Stella.

"Hey," she says, answering the phone. "Let me guess, you're wondering how my renovations are going."

"Indirectly, yes. You got time for a glass of wine?" I choke back a sob.

"Are you okay?" Concern seeps into her voice and I bite my lip to stop myself from crying.

"Yeah." I sniffle. "No."

"I think by 'glass' you meant 'bottle', right? Are you at home?"

"Yeah."

"I'm just finishing up at the office. I'll be over in half an hour."

I let out a sigh after I hang up the phone and stare blankly through the window. After a few minutes, I realize it's raining and I don't know how long I've been staring at the rain.

With a sigh, I peel myself off the couch and head to the bathroom. I take a long, hot shower and I curl up on the couch to wait for my friend. I feel numb. This morning, I was empowered. I was making the right decision.

But now? Now I don't know what to think. Martin came here—that must mean he cares about me, right? But then he just demanded I not quit like he owned me. He kissed me like I was his fucking property. Ever since the cabin, it feels like something between us has shifted. The intimacy is gone, but the intensity has remained. It leaves me alone and vulnerable and dirty.

When she rings the buzzer, I breathe a sigh of relief. I can't be alone right now. If I'm alone, I'm thinking about him, and if I'm thinking about him, I'm missing him. If I'm missing him, I'm hurting.

I open the door and Stella lifts up a bag. Bottles clank inside it and I try to smile.

"How many bottles did you bring?"

"Enough to make you forget about that bastard."

My eyebrows arch. "How did you know?"

Stella laughs, shaking her head. "Because it's always a bastard that makes us feel this way. Tell me everything. Wait, first—"

She twists off the top of a bottle and takes a swig. I crack a smile, and she hands it to me, nodding. I take a big gulp, wiping my lips and shaking my head.

"Feels like college all over again."

"That's the idea."

She goes to the kitchen and comes back with two glasses. "I guess we can pretend to be civilized." She grins and fills the glasses up to the brim.

Sensing that I'm not ready to talk, Stella tells me about her leaky roof and the sexy carpenter that came by to fix it.

"I can set you up with him, if you want." She swirls her wine and winks at me. "He's got all those great muscles that just scream 'manual labor'. Rough hands and a dirty mouth." She wiggles her eyebrows and I laugh. It feels like my face is cracking from the strain of smiling, but the pain in my heart eases.

"Sounds like you've already been there, done that."

"I wish," she says, snorting. "I'm working so many hours these days that I hardly even have the energy to pleasure myself, never mind someone else."

I snort sadly. My cheeks flush when I think of Martin in here, an hour ago, and how his touch made my panties soak through immediately. As much as I hated kissing him, my whole body responded to his touch as if he held the controls to my pleasure. My nipples hardened, and heat flooded my veins as soon as his hands were on me.

My mind and body were thrown into beautiful, irresistible chaos the second I saw him at my door.

But it was wrong. *He* is wrong!

"How about you, Nic? How's work? Did that bastard of a lawyer make it awful for you?"

"Pretty much... I quit this morning."

"What!" Her eyes widen. "Why?"

My throat gets tight and my eyes prickle. I bite my lip, taking a long, shuddering breath to steady myself. Stella puts a hand on my knee and I close my eyes.

"Remember how I told you that Martin and I stopped at the scene of the accident?"

"Mm-hmm."

"Well, I told him all about it. I told him about the hit and run, and how it was probably some drunk driver afraid of getting in trouble."

"Mm-hmm," she says, a bit more slowly. Her eyes are glued to me.

"Yesterday, he took a DUI case. The guy hit a woman and she's in the hospital now." I close my eyes, squeezing my wine glass so hard I'm afraid it might break.

"Oh, gosh. Oh, Nicole," Stella says, shaking her head. "Oh Nic, I'm sorry."

"I just don't know why he would do that. He said he didn't have a choice, but…"

"But you *always* have a choice."

"Exactly!"

"And you feel like he completely disregarded your feelings about this massive life event that you're just starting to process."

"Yes!"

"And you feel betrayed that he would let you open up to him and then stomp on your feelings."

"Yes! Is that so hard to understand?"

"Men are dense," she scoffs. "But even that I would expect them to get. Who is this guy anyway?"

"Martin Henderson. He's the youngest lawyer to ever make partner at Sanders & Perry, apparently."

"So he thinks he can walk on water," she says, rolling her eyes. "Figures."

I take a deep breath. "He showed up here today."

"No!" Her eyes widen. She takes a sip of wine without blinking or taking her eyes off me. I nod.

"Mm-hmm. Tried to kiss me."

"That *bastard!* Did you let him?"

"I was in shock, so yes." I blush. "Then I slapped him."

"No!" Stella says again, laughing. "You didn't!"

"I did."

Stella lets out a burst of laughter and throws her head back. She touches her glass to mine and arches her eyebrows. "Go you," she grins.

I laugh and then shake my head. "You know what the fucked-up thing is though? I actually *liked* it. I was turned on. I felt like my body was betraying me, like I should feel disgusted and violated, and I should never want his hands on me again. But I fucking *liked* it."

Stella takes a deep breath and shakes her head. "Been there. Maybe you should just hate-fuck him and get him out of your system."

"I'm not sure that's a good idea."

"It isn't. It will most definitely make things worse," she laughs. "But I haven't had sex in over six months, and a hate-fuck sounds pretty good to me right now."

We laugh, and I lean my head on Stella's shoulder. She fills up my wine glass again. I've missed this—actual human connection. What I have with Martin... it's hard to describe. It felt so deep and so real when we first started sneaking around, but then it just fell apart. I don't even know if I was imagining it from the start. Maybe he's just been a beautiful, empty shell of a human the whole time.

"What are you thinking about?" Stella pulls me out of my head, and I smile.

"I was just thinking that the one good thing to come out of all this was reconnecting with you. I'm getting along better with my sister, too. I'm starting to feel like myself again."

"I'm sorry I wasn't there for you." Stella's eyebrows draw together and she sighs. "I tried, but then... I guess I just stopped trying."

"I pushed everyone away." I stare at my wine. "You could have tried and tried and tried but it wouldn't have worked."

"I'm so sorry you went through all that. Jack was... he was great."

Grief starts raising its ugly head inside me and I shove it down. I'm sick of it. Sick of feeling weak and powerless. Sick of letting these feelings knock me down for days. Sick of it all.

I swallow past a lump in my throat and nod. "Yeah, he was."

"Hey!" Stella's eyes brighten. "How about I ask around at the office for a job for you? Maybe we could get you working at my firm. That would help ease the whole 'quitting because you fucked your boss' thing."

"I didn't quit because I fucked him," I grin.

"No, right. You quit because he's an ass, which only became a problem after you started fucking him." She arches an eyebrow and I laugh. "I'd say fucking him is one of the root causes. If we're being honest, that is."

I shake my head, grinning. "You know, one of the things I like most about you is also what I like the least about you."

"What's that?"

"Your ability to hold up a mirror to me and make me see what I don't want to see."

"Right now the mirror is saying your glass is empty," she grins, picking up the bottle again. "So what do you say? You want me to ask if they have a job for you?"

I take a deep breath and nod. "Sure. Yeah… that would be good, actually. That would make this whole thing a lot easier."

"As a bonus, it'll be that much easier to enlist you for my renovations."

"Or set me up with your sexy carpenter."

"I've decided he's mine," she laughs, shaking her head. "I'm calling dibs."

Stella refills our glasses, emptying the last drops of wine into her glass and cracking another bottle open. She leans back on my sofa and stares out the window.

"So… in all honesty, do you think it would be a really bad idea for me to sleep with my contractor?"

"No worse than me sleeping with my boss," I laugh. "So, I mean, go for it."

She nods and sips her wine. “Okay. I’ll do it. Are you going to hate-fuck your bastard lawyer boss?”

I take a deep breath and stare out the window with her. I shrug. “If the opportunity presents itself… maybe, yeah.” As soon as the words come out of my mouth, I know I wouldn’t have the heart to do it. Being that close to Martin would rip the heart clean out of my chest, but it feels good to pretend that it wouldn’t.

“Atta girl,” she chuckles. “Wouldn’t expect any less of you.”

26

MARTIN

I PACE up and down my apartment like a caged animal. My fists open and close constantly, and I run my fingers through my hair until it's sticking up in all directions. I stare out the floor-to-ceiling windows, seeing nothing.

Slumping down in an overstuffed armchair, I put my head in my hands.

I'm not sure what's worse—the guilt of knowing what I did to Nicole and her husband last January, or the thought of going to work when Nicole isn't there.

She made herself clear: she doesn't want to see me. She wants nothing to do with me.

I look down and realize my knee is bouncing up and down. My heel is hitting the hardwood floors, making a light tapping sound over and over and over. I haven't even taken my shoes off yet, and it sounds loud in my empty apartment.

The refrigerator suddenly stops making noise and I'm hit with the crushing realization that I'm alone.

Alone.

Again.

I let out a sigh and slump further down in the chair. My

shirt crumples underneath me and I know it'll crease, but I don't care. I don't care about anything except the look of hurt and betrayal in Nicole's eyes when I tried to kiss her.

If only she knew the truth—the whole truth—she'd be more hurt and betrayed than ever before.

My hand drifts to my chest and I clutch my heart. Every breath hurts. A crushing weight has installed itself on top of my chest and it isn't leaving.

How could I be so stupid? I let myself get vulnerable, something I'd promised I would never do. My eye catches a photo frame above the fireplace, and anger flares up inside me again. Jumping out of the chair, I take three long strides toward the photo frame. That's when it started. That photo is the exact moment where everything went wrong.

The moment when my life exploded into a million little pieces happened a week after that photo was taken. I can't handle it. I can't handle the hurt of what I've lost. I can't handle the guilt of what I've done. I can't handle the thought that I've hurt Nicole.

I grab the photo. The frame creaks under the force of my fingers and the need to just *break something* crashes into me. Starting in the pit of my stomach, it builds and builds until my thumb cracks the thin glass in front of the photo. Rage clouds my vision and a roar rumbles in my chest. With all my might, all my rage and hurt and guilt, I fling that fucking photo across the room. I don't flinch when it smashes against the wall, sprinkling glass all over my expensive hardwood floors.

My chest is heaving. My blood is thick and hot in my veins.

I stare at the broken photo. My shoes crunch on broken glass as I walk toward it. When I pick it up, I feel my heart harden a little bit more. It's turning to stone in my chest, and I welcome the emptiness that it leaves. I stare at the photo of Brianne and me. Her pregnant stomach was round and smooth and perfect. I was smiling in that picture. I was completely happy.

It feels like a stranger is staring back at me. That person doesn't exist anymore.

My breath slows back down to normal, and the pulse thundering in my ears dulls to a gentle thrum.

Sighing, I set the broken frame on the table. I crunch on more broken glass on my way to the cupboard to get the broom. As I clean up the broken glass, I'm embarrassed. Sweeping up the evidence of my rage makes me realize I lost control. I was weak.

Just like I have been with Nicole.

Weak and scared and pathetic.

Needy.

No, I need to get back to the real me. Back to the darkness that kept me warm when Brianne died. Back to the successful, uncompromising lawyer that her death created.

Back to myself.

I dump the broken glass in the garbage and slip the photo out of the broken frame. When I look at it, grief threatens to fill my heart again, so I slip the photo between the pages of a book and slide it on the bookshelf. Out of sight, and hopefully, never to be found again.

A MONTH LATER, when I get Julian's DUI case thrown out, Carmen shakes my hand. She's beaming, and I see something almost like admiration in her eyes.

I would be proud of myself, if I felt anything. Ever since that night, when I knew it was over between Nicole and me,

I've retreated back to the cold, empty loneliness inside myself.

"Good work, Marty," Carmen nods. "I'll be honest, I'm surprised you were able to pull it off."

"You shouldn't be."

"I guess I underestimated you."

"Another thing you shouldn't do."

She grins at me, and I walk out of the office with my head held high. When I get in my car, I glance in the back seat and see my duffle bag full of swimming gear. It's Tuesday, which is technically Nicole's day at the pool, but does she even still go?

I'm itching to let off some steam.

When Brianne died, I started working, and that was enough to fill the void. But now, even work doesn't make me forget. My muscles feel underused, and the pent-up energy inside me threatens to explode. No matter how much I work, and swim, and run, and lift weights, sleep has started to evade me. I'm lucky if I get two or three hours a night.

I know tonight will be no different. Unless I bring myself to the brink of exhaustion, I won't sleep.

So even though it's not my day at the pool, I shake my head.

"Fuck it," I say under my breath. Why am I still following that stupid schedule anyway? The pool doesn't belong to her. She probably doesn't even go anymore.

When I get there, my eyes scan the parking lot for her beat-up Honda. I don't see it, and I'm not sure if I'm relieved or disappointed. I grab my duffle bag and head inside.

It's not until I'm changed, showered, and swim capped that I see her. I've only seen her swimming a couple times, but I'd recognize her anywhere. She's in the slow lane, even though she's more than capable of being one of the faster ones. I stop walking, frozen in place as I watch her. When she nears the wall, I start walking again and slip into the lane next to hers.

I start swimming, and my muscles start burning. Every breath, every stroke, every kick—it all releases the tension in my body a little bit at a time.

But there's still a niggling feeling at the back of my neck. After a few lengths, I stop at the wall and poke my head out of the water.

"You're not supposed to be here," Nicole says beside me.

I turn to see her hanging on to the wall beside me. She's so close it makes my breath catch. Her goggles are propped up on her swim cap, and her face and shoulders are dotted with droplets of water. Her eyes, grey and steely, are trying their best to turn me to ice.

"Last time I checked, you don't own this place."

"We agreed on days."

"That was months ago, Nic."

"Don't call me Nic."

"What would you like me to call you?"

The lane rope bobs up and down between us as another swimmer does a turn behind me. He kicks and splashes both of us, but neither of us flinch.

She adjusts the strap of her bathing suit, and my body zings with heat. My cock throbs in my Speedos. Even the cold pool water can't stop the way I feel about her.

"I heard you got that singer off for the DUI."

"They didn't have a case against him."

"He *hit* a woman! She was in the hospital! Do you even know if she lived? Do you even care?" Her cheeks blush red and her eyes flash. The little specks of green around the edges sparkle with anger.

"She's fine," I lie. Both her legs were broken, and she's not in good shape. Guilt needles at my heart and I huff. I pull my goggles back down over my face. "It was great to see you, Nic. Always a pleasure."

I kick off the wall and swim away from her. It's all I can do to get away from those eyes, those lips, those hands. Another second beside her and I would have tried to kiss her again.

If I was trying to prove to myself that she no longer holds any power over me, I failed.

27

NICOLE

I WATCH him swim away as the anger boils in the pit of my stomach. My whole body tingles with heat and anger and desire, and I hate myself for it.

I shouldn't want him. I should despise him!

Pulling myself out of the pool, I stomp toward the change rooms. I can't be near him. I can't believe he thought it was okay to share the pool with me. Of *course* he would. Arrogant, no-good, cocky *asshole*!

Tears sting my eyes and I brush them away. I wish I could run to the changing room and hide in a shower stall, but my wet feet and the tiles around the pool are slippery, so all I can manage is an awkward waddle. As soon as I make it around the corner, I grab my bag and go to a shower.

I turn the water on as hot as it'll go and stand under the stream. I won't let myself cry. I'm done crying.

Why would I let him have that much power over me? It was a silly fling, and it's over. I have a new job, new coworkers, and hopefully at some point, I'll meet someone new. I'm not crying over him. I refuse.

I wash my swim cap, my goggles, and I rinse my bathing

suit as I wear it. Then, I take it off and take a long, hot shower. By the time I'm done, I feel almost normal again.

Taking my time getting dressed, I pull out my makeup bag and swipe some mascara over my lashes. I brush my hair and then take a deep breath.

Even after everything, I still want him to think I'm pretty.

Pathetic.

Gathering my things, I take a deep breath and step out of the changing room.

My timing could not have been worse. Martin pulls himself out of the pool just as I step out. Water runs down his chiseled body—a body that I used to worship. It drops off him, carving every valley of muscle along his arms, his chest, his abs. I watch as a droplet of water speeds down his obliques toward his tiny Speedos.

Toward his bulge.

My eyes dart back up to see him pull off his goggles and swim cap. He shakes his head like a dog, and then starts walking toward his towel.

That's when he spots me. My eyes widen and I put my head down, speeding toward the exit.

"Nicole!" He says, jogging after me. "Nic, wait!"

The lifeguard's whistle rings out. "No running!" She yells. Martin ignores her. I look over my shoulder to see him slip and lose his balance. He wobbles but is able to right himself.

"You're going to break your neck," I say, turning toward him. "Not that I would care."

"I don't care. Just... slow down. Please talk to me."

Water drips from his wet hair onto his muscular shoulders. I force myself not to drop my gaze. Instead, I stare at the wall and bite my lip. He takes a step toward me, and my heart speeds up.

"Nicole," he says softly.

"What?"

"I'm sorry."

His voice is so gentle that it makes me look at him again. His deep, ocean-blue eyes stare into mine. His palms turn toward me and he shakes his head.

"I shouldn't have taken the case."

"No, you shouldn't have. Especially not right after I opened up to you about Jack."

His face twists and he looks away from me. "I have to tell you something."

I frown as the air between us thickens. He's still staring at a spot on the floor, and I let my eyes drift over his body. I miss it. I miss the way he smelled and tasted. I miss the way his chest would rumble when I did something to turn him on. I miss *him*. I haven't been with anyone—or even flirted with anyone, really—since we split up. There are a couple men who have made advances toward me once I started working at Stella's firm, but I've just ignored it.

I'm not ready.

But now, as I stare at this perfect man—the man that I thought I almost loved—I know that I still want him.

I take a step toward him and raise my hand toward his chest, then hesitate. My hand hovers an inch from his skin and I drop it.

I'm not going to make the same mistakes over and over. I clench my jaw and force myself to look him in the eye.

"What do you need to tell me?"

His eyes turn back toward me and the pain I see in them is staggering. My heart breaks for him, and all I want to do is throw my arms around his neck and tell him that whatever it is, it's okay.

He opens his mouth, but no words come out. His eyebrows draw together on his forehead, and the intensity of his gaze increases. He closes his eyes for a moment, and all the breath leaves his body. His shoulders fall, and he shakes his head. When he opens his eyes again, they're clearer, but the sadness remains.

"I miss you," he finally says. "I've missed you every day since the day you quit."

Velvety, soft butterfly wings tickle the corners of my heart. My legs shake.

I hate it. I hate the power he has over me.

I don't know what to say. I want to scream that I've missed him too. I want to tell him that I hate him, and I love him, and everything in between. I want to say that it hurts to look at him, but the thought of never seeing him again makes me feel even worse.

I don't say anything, though. I just lift my fingers up and brush them along his jaw. He closes his eyes and exhales softly, leaning into my touch.

"I miss you too," I whisper.

His eyes darken with desire, and a current of electricity zips down my spine. He cups my cheek in his hand.

"I'm sorry," he whispers.

"I know."

Then, he brings his lips to mine.

The last time we kissed, it was intense and angry and wrong. This time, it feels like the rightest thing in the world. His lips are soft, and they taste like chlorine. When he parts my lips and slips his tongue between them, he tastes like himself. Like heaven and earth and love and hate and everything that's ever meant anything to me.

He kisses me gently, his hand tilting my face up toward him. He's trembling, holding me like I'm a china doll that he might break if he's too rough.

Maybe that's exactly what I am.

His tongue swipes across my lower lip. I deepen the kiss, standing up on my tiptoes to kiss him harder. I wrap my arms around his neck as the water on his body soaks into my clothes. I shiver, melting into him and I know that he's the man for me.

Even with a month apart, even as I hated every fiber of his being, even as I thought the worst of him, he's the only one that I wanted.

When he pulls away, his eyes are cloudy. He rests his forehead against mine and lets out a breath.

"I'm going to go get dressed. Will you wait for me?"

I nod, because my voice is gone. I walk out of the pool area, suddenly aware of how many people must have seen us. Who cares? My heart is beating again and I feel alive. I shuffle away from it all, heading toward the lobby. I lean against the wall and wait.

When he comes back out, my breath catches in my throat. His broad shoulders stretch the fabric of his white tee-shirt, and his dark jeans hang off his slim hips. His beauty is breathtaking and my heart shatters all over again. He smiles at me, extending his hand.

"Will you come to my place?"

"Sure." I slip my fingers into his.

"Where's your car?"

I chew my lip, shaking my head. "It broke down. I'm saving up to have it fixed, but..." I trail off. "I took the bus."

His eyebrows draw together and he nods. He pulls his keys out and presses a button to unlock the doors. Opening my door for me, he helps me into his car. His hand presses on the small of my back and happiness floods through me.

Is it happiness? Right now, happiness and desire feel very similar.

He jogs around the back of the car and gets in the driver's

seat. Before turning on the keyless ignition, he turns toward me and pulls me in for a kiss. He groans into my mouth, scraping his teeth over my lower lip and kissing me harder. His hand drifts down my neck and over my chest. My nipples harden under my shirt as his hand brushes across them. I moan, kissing him harder.

"You're irresistible, Nicole," he breathes, and my heart thunders.

28

MARTIN

I OPEN my front door for Nicole. She steps through, smiling shyly.

"Haven't been here in a while," she says, glancing around. "It looks the same." She has her back to me, staring out the windows at the Denver skyline.

I snake my arms around her waist and bury my face in her dark hair. I inhale the fresh, fruity scent of her shampoo and groan.

"You always smell so good."

She laughs, turning her head toward me. "You clearly haven't spent enough time with me. I promise you I get stinky."

My heart thuds and I look her in the eye. "No, I haven't spent enough time with you. Eternity wouldn't be long enough."

Somewhere in the deep recesses of my mind, I know I need to tell her the truth about the accident. I need to come clean. But right now, with my arms around her, and her perky little ass pressing back into my cock... now is not the time.

My hand moves up to cup her breast, and she exhales.

She turns her head toward me and I catch her lips in mine. Moving her hips back and forth, she makes my already-hard cock throb. She moans into my mouth, and I kiss her harder.

I claw at her shirt, bringing it up to her chin so I can feel her silky soft skin. I groan again.

"I've missed the feel of your skin," I growl.

"That's what someone with a taxidermy fetish would say."

"Only you could come out with a line like that at a moment like this."

She spins in my arms, grinning. "What's a moment like this?"

"It's the moment where I remind you that you're mine. You always were, and you always will be."

Her eyes widen, and her legs quiver. I drop my hand between them, feeling the heat of her desire. I sigh as I imagine how wet her panties must be right now.

Stroking my hand back and forth, I run my lips over her neck. "You hear me, Nicole? You're mine. Mine to touch, mine to hold, mine to fuck."

She exhales, rolling her hips toward me. "I'm yours."

"Don't you ever forget it again," I growl. Nicole hooks her arms around my neck, staring me straight in the eye. She kisses me gently, just barely brushing her lips against mine. I curl my hand over her pants as she presses her center toward me.

"I missed you," she breathes. "I missed you so much."

"I know."

I can't wait any longer. I unbutton her jeans and rip them down her legs. She gasps, kicking off her shoes and helping me take her pants off all the way. I pick her up, kissing her hard. She wraps her legs around my waist and I feel her soaked panties resting against my crotch. I groan as the pressure in the pit of my stomach builds.

"I want you," she breathes between kisses.

"Not yet," I growl. Carrying her to the bedroom, I toss her down on the bed. With a flick of my wrist, I tear her panties off and dive head-first into her pussy.

The gasps and moans that she emits almost make me cream my pants. Her hips buck and her back arches toward me, and I just lick, and suck, and taste her until her whole body vibrates.

Her orgasm tastes better than I remembered. I moan into her slit, driving my tongue in and out of her as she comes. She curls her fingers into my hair, screaming my name over and over.

I don't give her a chance to recover. I've waited too long and dreamt of her too many times. I need her. I stand up and kick my pants off before ripping my shirt off over my head. Nicole scrambles to take the rest of her clothes off, and then our eyes meet for a brief moment.

Her dark hair is wild. Her eyes glint with desire and she sucks her bottom lip into her mouth. My eyes travel down her body and I exhale slowly.

"You're so beautiful, Nic."

Instead of responding, she just opens her arms toward me. I reach for the nightstand where I keep my condoms and pull one out. I have it out of the wrapper and in front of my cock when her hand reaches out and stops me. I look at her, frowning.

"I..." She takes a sharp breath in. "I want to feel you. All of you."

My eyes widen, and I nod. "Okay."

I drop the condom as all my blood rushes to my cock. I can't think of anything else, only sheathing myself inside her. My lips meet hers as I spread her thighs with my knees. She hooks her ankles around my back, tilting her hips toward me.

The tip of my cock brushes against her slit, and I groan. I move back and forth, leaning my forehead against hers. I close my eyes and exhale.

"That feels so fucking good."

"I know," she says.

Her velvety smoothness feels better than I could have imagined. I can't hold back any longer. Entering her slowly, I feel her walls stretch to accept me. Inch by inch, I plunge my cock deep inside her. We both exhale, and I groan.

"Nicole..."

"Yeah?"

"Fuck," I manage to say. "You feel so fucking good. You're so tight."

She smiles, biting her lip. "Well there hasn't been anything up there in a while..."

My heart thumps. For the past month, the thought of Nicole with other men has been driving me wild. On sleepless nights, when I've stared at the ceiling and it's stared right back at me, I've imagined Nicole tangled in the bedsheets with someone else. The rage that those thoughts ignited in me is almost indescribable.

But now I know that she's mine. I know that my cock is the only cock that will ever be inside her, and I know that she's the only one that I want. Warmth explodes in my chest. She curls her fingers into my hair, rolling her hips toward me once more.

"I think I'm in love with you," I blurt out, and I drive my cock inside her.

Nicole laughs, and then gasps when my cock plunges deeper. "You did *not* just say that for the first time while we're having sex."

"What's wrong with that?" I say, thrusting again. She

gasps, closing her eyes. Her hands dig into my hair and I drive my cock even deeper.

Watching the pleasure wash over her is more erotic than anything I can explain. Her walls grip my shaft tighter, and I know that I won't last long.

As our motions become faster, and more frantic, Nicole opens her eyes.

"I think I love you too."

I explode.

I fill her up completely with my seed, groaning as my orgasm takes over my entire body. I shake, tense, contract, and finally relax as she gasps underneath me. Her hands drift up and down my back and I finally collapse on top of her.

When I slide off her, I roll onto my back and exhale. She turns toward me, putting her hand on my chest.

"Your heart is racing."

"Yeah," I reply.

She bites her lip. "Did you mean it? What you said?"

I turn my head to look at her beautiful face. "Yes. Did you?"

She nods. "I think so."

I grin. "You think so?"

"Take what you can get, buddy," she laughs, and then I pull her in for a kiss.

29

NICOLE

SOMETIME LATER, when sleep starts to creep up on me, Martin shifts beside me. The mattress dips as he turns, and he lets out a big sigh.

"You okay?"

"Yeah."

I open my eyes and see him staring at the ceiling. A vein in his jaw is twitching, and he swallows thickly. I prop myself up on my elbow and put a hand on his chest.

"Are you sure you're okay?"

"I need to tell you something."

Right away, I know something's wrong. The hairs on the back of my neck prickle, and my chest is suddenly hollow. I swallow, trying to bring back a bit of moisture to my suddenly dry mouth.

"Okay," I say. I rub my eyes and sit up.

Martin's face twists, and he shakes his head.

"I'm sorry. I just want you to know that from the bottom of my heart, I'm sorry."

My heart hammers, and panic starts to claw at my throat. An hour ago, he was telling me he loved me. And now...? I blink, pulling my hand away from his chest. He turns toward me and I see the same pain in his eyes that I saw the day he tried to kiss me at my apartment.

"Did you sleep with someone else or something? I mean, we weren't together, so..."

He shakes his head, snorting.

"Sleep with someone else? God, I tried. Many times. I could never go through with it. Ever since you stole my parking space, it's always been you. Only you."

I consider making a comment about it not being his parking space to lighten the mood, but I bite my tongue. It's not the time. This feels significant. It feels scary.

He takes a deep, rattling breath.

"Do you remember how I told you my wife died?"

"She had to have an emergency C-section, right?"

He nods, turning back toward the ceiling. His eyes go hazy, as if he's being transported back to that time. "We'd been trying to have a kid for years," he says. His voice sounds hollow. "She was going through IVF treatments, and finally, *finally*, we had a baby."

He inhales again, squeezing his eyes shut. A tear rolls down the side of his face, and I wipe it away with the backs of my fingers.

"It was the happiest time of my life. And then, when I was over in Golden for a case, she started bleeding. A lot. I couldn't get back fast enough, because Carmen had sent me to the fucking mountains, so Jaime took her to the hospital. They couldn't save the baby, and—" he sobs. My heart shatters for him. I put my hand on his shoulder, stroking him softly. A lump forms in my throat as I see this man—this beautiful, stoic man—break down.

I wish I could take some of his pain away and shoulder it

myself. I wish I could mend his heart, soothe him and love him until he was whole again.

"By the time they took the baby out, she'd lost so much blood. She was unconscious, and they tried to revive her. They gave her blood. They tried, and she hung on for a long time—almost a week."

He stops talking, and I squeeze his shoulder. This is the most he's told me about his wife's death. Tears run down my cheeks and I let them fall off my chin onto the blanket.

Martin takes a deep breath. "On the day that it happened, I was in Golden."

"For work."

He nods. "Jaime called me from the hospital, and I started panicking. I got back as quickly as I could but I..." He takes a deep breath. "I got in an accident on the way home."

My heart starts beating. I think I know what he's going to say, but I don't want to hear it. My mind starts heading for the abyss, and the darkness begins sucking me in.

No.

No, no, no.

It's not true.

"I was driving on the I-70," he says, turning his head toward me. In his eyes, I see pain, and something else. I see guilt. "I hit a car. I side-swiped it. I saw it spin into the other lane, and I thought they would be okay. I needed to get back to Brianne. I..."

His face crumples and he starts to cry.

"I'm so sorry, Nicole. I'm so fucking sorry. I should have stopped."

I shake my head. "No." I back away from him, shaking my head faster. "No, no, no, no, no."

Scrambling up from the bed, I back up until I hit the far wall. My fingernails scratch on the wall behind me as I try to make sense of what he's just told me. He stares at me, his eyes hollow. He extends his hands toward me and I wrap my own arms around my naked body.

"I'm so sorry, Nicole. I thought someone would see you. I was a mess. I knew Brianne was in trouble, I—"

"Do *not* try to garner sympathy by using your fucking dead wife," I spit. The darkness swallows me whole. "You liar. You monster. You *murderer*!"

He's crying, but I don't care. I feel dirty and foolish. My heart implodes, and shards of it embed themselves in my flesh. My whole body hurts. I'm in agony. I scramble to pick up my clothes, shaking. Martin stands up, and I just point my trembling finger at him.

"Take one step toward me and I'm calling the police."

"Nic—"

"*Get away from me!*" My voice is guttural and animalistic. It's not my voice, it's all my pain and my grief and my horror ripping through my vocal cords. I grab my throat, struggling for a breath.

His face twists some more, and he sits down on the bed with his head in his hands. I get dressed as I hyperventilate. By the time I've gathered my things, my whole world has tilted on its axis. I pause in the doorway to the bedroom and turn around.

Martin is still sitting on his bed—the bed where we just had sex—with his head in his hands. He's naked, and pathetic, and weak.

"How long have you known?"

He turns to look at me, and I don't recognize the shell of a man that meets my eye. I stand up straighter, willing my lower lip not to tremble.

"Since you showed me the scene of the accident."

I stare at the ceiling to try to stop my tears, but they pour out of my eyes. "And you still had sex with me? You still took that DUI case? You told me you *loved* me?"

"Nicole, I—"

I put up my hand, shaking my head. I don't want to hear it. I don't want to hear the voice that I've been missing for the past month. I don't want to hear his story of heartbreak and grief. I don't want to think that the man that I thought I was falling in love with is the man who killed my husband.

I look at him once more. He opens his mouth to speak, but we just stare at each other in silence. Tears flow down my cheeks, but I hold my chin up high.

I may be emotional, but I am not weak. I turn my back to him and walk out of his apartment.

I walk for ten, fifteen, maybe twenty minutes. I'm not sure how long. There are no taxis in sight, and the crushing weight of Martin's confession hits me like a speeding train. I sit down on the curb and I cry.

When a cab finally comes into view, I stand up and wave it down. I wipe my eyes and nose on my sleeve and take a deep breath before getting in and giving him my address.

"Everything okay?" The cabbie asks as he glances at me through the rear-view mirror.

"Yeah," I say. "Everything's fine."

30

MARTIN

I DON'T KNOW how long I sit there. I hear the door close and it rattles my bones. Then, I just sit on the edge of my bed with my head in my hands and let all the emotion drain from my body until I'm empty. Finally, when my body starts shivering, I realize that I'm cold.

My skin is covered in goosebumps, and my cock has shriveled up to the size of my thumb. My muscles creak as I stand up, and I shuffle to the shower. The water hits my body and warms it up, and I just stand there, unfeeling.

Mechanically, I turn the water off and dry myself. I slip into some sweat pants and lie on my bed, but then I turn to the side and realize that Nicole was there. The imprint of her body is still on the sheets, and I can smell the scent of her shampoo on the pillow.

My chest squeezes. I grab my pillow and head for the couch. I take a couple sleeping pills and collapse on the cushions.

Dawn is breaking when I wake up. The sun is shining on a beautiful summer's day. I groan. The fact that the world is still turning is a slap in the face.

Just like when Brianne died, I feel like the world is spinning around me. My world is falling to pieces, but somehow, unaware, life for everyone else goes on.

Everything aches when I sit up on the couch. I stare at the pillow, and then at the rug, and finally push myself up to get a cup of coffee. I groan as I stand, as if my body's aged fifty years overnight. Even the soles of my feet hurt. I hobble to the kitchen and make a cup of coffee, and then I stand at the counter and drink it.

Somehow, I make it to work. I head for my office and close the door, sitting behind my desk and staring at my blank screen. My eyes drift to the edge of my desk, where I made Nicole orgasm the very first time. My chest feels like it has a bloody axe embedded in it, and the ugly truth starts to creep up on me.

She's right. I'm a piece of shit. I lied to her—lied by omission. I should have told her when we stopped at that damn tree. I should have broken down and begged for her forgiveness. I should have turned myself in, and then gotten down on my knees and begged her not to hate me.

But I didn't.

I said nothing. I let her believe that the loss of her husband reminded me of my wife, when all it did was remind me of my guilt.

Kelly pokes her head in the door with a list of messages. Her eyes widen when she sees my face, and I wonder how bad I really look. It's not like I looked at myself in the mirror this morning. I can't face myself.

She slides through the doorway and pads toward me. She places the messages on my desk, along with an envelope with our firm's name emblazoned on it.

I nod. "Thanks, Kelly."

She hesitates. "Martin... Are you okay?"

I must look pretty fucking bad.

"I'm fine. Cancel my appointments this morning and don't bother me with anything."

She nods and walks out without saying anything. As soon as the door closes, I exhale. I stare at my blank screen again, and the stack of papers on the edge of my desk. I can't bring myself to even turn on my computer right now.

Instead, I reach for the envelope. The page inside is made with thick, expensive-feeling paper. I already know what the letter says—I've gotten a number of them in the past year. I read it, and my heart sinks.

It's a bonus for winning the DUI case. For our high-profile clients, the firm reserves part of the fees as incentives if we win the cases. Usually, a letter like this would fill me with pride, and I'd buy myself something nice. The first time, it was a new car. The second time, I bought a new entertainment system for my apartment.

But now?

Now I toss the letter aside and drop my head in my hands. I feel dirty. That letter just reinforces that I'm a liar, and a piece of shit. I don't deserve a bonus. I should be in jail.

A tear drops onto the letter, and that's when I realize I'm crying. Once I start, I can't stop. Tears keep coming and coming and coming and I sob. My shoulders shake and I rock back and forth. I'm not sure how long I cry, but eventually the tears slow down. My throat feels raw, and my body feels like an empty husk.

I stare at the letter. My eyes drift down to Carmen's signature at the bottom, and my heart hardens. I know what I need to do.

I pick up the letter with the tips of my fingers as I stand up. Running my fingers through my hair, I take a deep breath and head for the door. I ignore the shocked looks and whispers as I walk across the office. I just keep my eyes on my destination.

When I open Carmen's door, she looks up. Her eyebrows arch, and she slides her glasses off her face. She stands up, walking around her desk.

"Marty," she says. "What's going on?"

I close the door and look her in the eye. She takes a tentative step toward me. She looks concerned—she probably should. I'm on the verge of a fucking mental breakdown. She's my boss, my mentor, the woman who gave me all my opportunities in this career. She's a tough, strong woman, but now, she takes another step toward me and slides her hand over my arm.

"Marty," she says. Her voice is softer than I've ever heard it. She leads me to a chair, her eyes not leaving my face.

I hand her the letter and struggle to swallow. I take a deep breath. Her eyes don't leave my face.

"Carmen, I need to tell you something."

"Okay," she says evenly.

I thought telling the story a second time would be easier. It's not. With another deep breath, I straighten my shoulders and for the first time, I face my past and my future head-on.

"A year and a half ago, I was involved in a hit and run."

Her eyes widen. "Oh my God," she sighs. "Did they ever find the guy?"

I shake my head. "I'm the guy. I hit a car, and I didn't stop. Brianne had just been taken to the hospital, and—" My voice cracks, and I take a deep breath to steady it. "I found out that the driver of the other car died."

"Fuck," she breathes, dropping her head. "Fuck, Marty."

"I'm going to turn myself in."

"What?"

"I can't handle it anymore. I can't do it."

"Marty..."

"I need to do it, Carmen."

She puts a hand on my knee. "Just take a deep breath, Martin."

Frustration flares up inside me. She's not listening to me! I didn't come here to be placated, or to be convinced otherwise. I just came here to confess. I came here to come clean.

"Look at me." Her voice is hard, and I find myself doing as she says. "We are going to deal with this. You have a bright future ahead of you, and I don't want you to throw it all away."

"It was wrong, Carmen. I killed someone."

"Your wife was dying."

"And I killed a man."

"Stop it."

My lip trembles, and I hate the fact that I'm falling to pieces in front of my boss.

"Just give me a week, Marty," she says. I don't want to, but I feel weak. I want to relinquish control of the situation. I want someone else to tell me what the right thing to do is. I don't want to wrestle with my conscience anymore.

I'm tired.

I'm weak.

I'm alone.

Carmen squeezes my knee and stares me straight in the eye. "Don't do anything stupid, Henderson. You hear me?"

I nod. "Okay."

"Take the rest of the day off."

"I don't need to—"

"Do it." She puts up a hand to stop my protest. "I'll come up with a plan."

"Carmen, you're not listening. I don't want a plan. I want to turn myself in."

"Don't let one mistake ruin your life, Martin."

My chest heaves. I look at my boss, shaking my head. The guilt and sadness open up inside me like a bottomless void. I stand on the edge of the abyss, and I hear myself chuckle bitterly.

"It already has."

31

NICOLE

One month later...

Stella was right, having a routine helped. I took a day off after that awful night at Martin's house. That evening, Stella nearly knocked down my door to find out what was wrong. She got me into the shower and made me dinner. She picked me up the next morning and stayed with me for the first couple nights.

She said she needed somewhere to stay because of the renovations at her house, but I know it was because she was afraid to leave me alone.

It took me ten days to tell her what happened. She was so angry her whole face went red, and she started shaking. She crumpled a bunch of papers and shouted about suing the bastard, but that only made me cry.

The rest of the time has been a blur. I've gotten up, gone to work, eaten, and slept. Last week, I even started swimming again.

Martin tried calling me a couple times, but I blocked his number and redirected all his emails to my spam folder. I deleted him on social media, but I was still reminded of him everywhere I went. My heart still skips a beat every time a black BMW passes me in the street.

The days are okay. The worst time is nighttime. I try to tire myself out enough that I'm asleep before my head hits the pillow, but it doesn't always work.

Tonight, I'm staring at the ceiling again as my thoughts swirl around me. It's almost too easy to give in to the anger, the outrage, the deep, unending sadness.

So, I try to fight it. I close my eyes and take deep breaths. I count my inhales up to five, and then exhale up to five. I do this over and over until my mind clears.

I open my eyes when my phone dings. I turn to my nightstand and check my phone, frowning at the notification. It's an app I use to track my menstrual cycle.

Your period is 7 days late, it says.

I frown. It's been giving me these notifications every day. For some reason, tonight's notification makes me pause. My period hasn't been late since I was in my teens. I put my hand on my stomach and take a deep breath.

I won't let my mind go there. I won't let myself think about what it means for my period to be late.

I'm on the pill! I get up and check my pill package. I'm on the sugar pills, so I should be bleeding by now. My period week is nearly over. I flip the package over and frown.

Then, my eyes widen. Stamped in the bottom corner of the packaging is a faint expiration date... from two years ago. I take three quick, staggered breaths. Maybe it's some weird European date format that's all out of order—but the year is still two years ago. Maybe it's wrong. Maybe...

I pull up the internet on my phone and search for an explanation. With every new search result, my heart sinks further and further down. Pregnant, pregnant, pregnant.

Shaking, panting, with panic rising inside me, I throw my phone aside.

It's not true.

It can't be.

It's impossible.

I squeeze my eyes shut and count my breaths again until my heart slows down. Then, I stare at the expired package of pills again and try not to cry.

THE NEXT MORNING, the first thing I do is go to the bathroom. My eyes prickle when there's still no sign of Aunt Flo. I sit on the toilet, taking deep breaths and staring at the ceiling.

When I get dressed, I wince as I put my bra on. My breasts feel swollen and sensitive, just like they have been for the past two weeks. How did I not notice that before? I poke them and cup them, frowning. They feel heavier than usual, and my nipples are so sensitive even the soft fabric of my bra feels rough.

I shake my head, ignoring the voice in the back of my head that's screaming the obvious to me.

I delete the period tracking app and try to ignore it, but anxiety starts mounting inside me. Stella notices something's wrong, and she pulls me aside at work. I make up some excuse about sleeping poorly. She frowns but says nothing.

It takes me three days to work up the courage to buy a pregnancy test. When I'm in the pharmacy, I feel strangely ashamed. I'm a grown woman, and pregnancy should be a joyous, natural thing. Instead, I'm buying a bunch of stuff I don't need to cover up the fact that I'm really here to see if there's a baby growing inside me.

The pregnancy test feels like a ticking time bomb. As

soon as I unwrap it and pee on the end of it, it might blow my whole world apart.

The test says to wait until morning, and I toss and turn all night. When I finally wake up, bleary-eyed and tired, I stumble to the bathroom and frown at the box. My heart hammers as I unwrap it and sit down on the toilet, and I bite my lip to keep myself from crying.

I start the timer on my phone and turn the test around. I brush my teeth and start getting ready for work to ignore the explosion that's about to rock my world to pieces.

When the timer goes off and I turn the test around, I'm not even surprised. It doesn't feel like an explosion. Two little blue lines stare back at me, clear and strong.

I'm pregnant.

I sit down on the floor and stare at the test. Then, I get up, throw the test in the garbage and keep getting ready for work.

Around lunchtime, Stella comes to my desk and invites me out for some food. I follow her mechanically, putting one step in front of the other. She's talking about something, but I don't hear a word. I don't even know if I've gotten any work done.

Finally, when we sit down to eat, she looks at me for the first time.

"Honey, what's wrong? You look like you just saw a ghost."

I stare at my sandwich. "I'm pregnant."

Her jaw drops and her eyes widen. "Are you sure?"

I nod.

"How? I thought you were on the pill."

"They're expired."

"What?" I look up to see her wide-eyed. "What do you mean? How long have you had them?"

I sigh, shaking my head. "I don't know. I had an old pack from back before Jack and I were trying for a baby, but I thought I was using the new one I just got. Maybe they got mixed up in my medicine cabinet. I don't know. I don't know... I just... I don't know."

"Okay, honey. That's okay." She puts her hand over mine and I take deep, calming breaths. "Are you... How do you feel? Are you... happy?"

That makes me laugh. I laugh and laugh and laugh, and Stella looks at me like I've lost my mind. Maybe I have. Finally, I wipe my eyes and shake my head.

"No, Stella. I'm not happy. The man who killed my husband impregnated me right before he told me what he did. I'm alone, I'm depressed, I'm broke, and I have no prospects at happiness or financial stability."

Stella stares at the table between us. Her body is vibrating and she shakes her head. "Fuck, Nic."

"Yeah."

"Are you going to keep it?"

She looks up at me, her eyebrows drawing together.

I chuckle bitterly, shaking my head. "That's the thing that's fucking with my head, Stella. I want it. I want to keep it. I want to have a baby, and I want to love it and be the best mom ever." I put my hand to my stomach as tears start welling in my eyes. "And the most fucked up part of me wants to have a piece of Martin with me. I know he's horrible, and awful, but... I don't even know. I can't explain it."

Stella reaches across the table and takes my other hand in hers. "That's not fucked up, Nic. That's beautiful."

"I feel like I should hate this baby, but I don't. I'm so confused."

"You shouldn't hate the baby," she says, grinning. "The baby did nothing wrong."

"I just... When Jack died, I thought my chances at a family died with him. And then when Martin and I imploded, I..." I look at her, begging her with my eyes to understand. "But now..."

"You have another chance."

I nod. "I'm terrified."

She squeezes my hand. "Are you going to tell him?"

I take a deep breath, staring at my stomach. If I tell him, he'd probably help me out financially. I'd have a bit of support and logistically, it would be easier. He's the father, and he probably has a right to know. But if I tell him, it means I have to talk to him. It means he'll be in my life forever, and I don't know if I can handle that.

Stella squeezes my hand again and I look up at her. I shrug. "I don't know."

32

MARTIN

"YOU'RE a hard man to get a hold of," the woman says when I walk into the conference room. She extends her hand to shake mine, but her eyes remain hard.

She's got deep, red hair and piercing green eyes. Her face is angular and quite beautiful, but it lacks the softness of Nicole's features. I take a deep breath, mentally smacking myself. I shouldn't be thinking of Nicole.

"What can I help you with? I don't think we've met, Mrs...?"

"King. Stella King."

"What can I do for you, Ms. King?"

She takes a seat, straightening her silk blouse. She folds her manicured hands on the table in front of her and looks me up and down.

"I'm here unofficially," she starts. My eyebrows arch, and she holds my gaze. "My dear friend and coworker is a former, uh, *acquaintance* of yours."

"Oh?"

She clears her throat. "Nicole Martinez."

Years of training allow me to keep my face steady. A lump

forms in my throat, and I try to swallow. Stella's eyes narrow, and she shakes her head.

"I thought you'd be taller."

"I'm six-three."

She shrugs. "I don't know. I guess I just expected... I don't know what I expected." She waves her hands in my direction. "I expected *more*."

"Why exactly are you here?"

"Why exactly aren't you in jail?"

My pulse quickens and I stand up. My chair rolls back behind me and I clear my throat. "I've had enough of this. If you're just here to waste my time and make idle threats—"

"She's pregnant."

I waver. I lean on the table to support myself, because the ground has suddenly turned to jelly. My heart falls out my ass and my vision starts to blur at the edges. I focus on the woman across from me, blinking rapidly as the words sink in.

"She's p... she's preg..."

"Pregnant, yes." Stella arches her eyebrow. She shakes her head, putting her hand to her forehead. "I shouldn't be here. I've overstepped. Fuck," she breathes. "She's going to kill me."

"No, wait," I say as she stands up. "Wait, I just..."

We stare at each other for a few moments. I'm afraid to move from the table in case I fall over. The ground is heaving underneath me, and my vision isn't exactly clear. I take a deep breath, focusing on Stella's green eyes until I regain my balance.

"She told me she was on the pill," I finally manage to say. "We used a condom all the other times... just... how?"

Stella sighs. She shakes her head and looks at me with something new in her eyes—is it pity?

"I thought you had a right to know, but I don't know

anymore. What you did to her is inexcusable. I shouldn't have come here. I've made a mistake."

"I'm ashamed of myself," I blurt out as she reaches the conference room door. She turns her head toward me and stares me down with those green orbs of hers.

Finally she nods. "You should be."

When the door closes behind her, I collapse onto a chair. I groan as my stomach twists. Leaning my head back on the chair, I close my eyes and try to take deep, calming breaths. My heart isn't getting the memo, because it's still bouncing around my ribcage like I just injected adrenaline.

Carmen appears in the doorway. She steps inside and closes the door behind her. Standing in front of me, she stares at me with her arms crossed.

"What was that about?"

"Nothing," I say. I'm not ready to talk about it.

"You remember the plan, right? I've seen that look on your face before. This is about the accident, isn't it?"

"No."

"Then it's about Nicole."

"Carmen..."

Her eyes narrow. For the past month, she's been working on burying the hit and run. She's manufactured an alibi for me, complete with falsified documents and plane tickets. My stomach turns again, and I shake my head.

"I can't do it, Carmen."

"I've put everything on the line for you, Martin," she says, her voice tense. "Everything. I've bent my morals so far I'm surprised they haven't snapped in half."

I shake my head. "I'm sorry. I've done too much wrong. I can't keep running. I can't hide. Not anymore. I can't put you in this position; I could ruin everything for you."

She stares at me for a few moments. I watch her swallow

and then turn away from me without a word. I pull out my phone and try to call Nicole for the thousandth time. For the thousandth time, it beeps and tells me the phone number is disconnected. I try every social media outlet I can think of, but I can't find her anywhere. I send her yet another email that I know she probably won't see.

I need to talk to her.

The need grows and grows inside me until I find myself jogging to my car. By the time I pull up outside Nicole's building, my pulse is thundering in my ears and my palms are sweaty. I go to the buzzer, mashing it over and over. I imagine the buzzer ringing in an empty apartment, and my shoulders slump.

The door opens behind me and an old woman steps out.

"Do you know Nicole Martinez?" I pounce on her, breathless. "Does she still live here?"

The woman looks at me suspiciously. My eyes dart from her to the door, and I run my fingers through my hair. My tie is undone and I probably look like I'm on the verge of insanity.

"She moved out last week," the woman finally says through tight lips. She holds her jacket closed at the neck, looking down her nose at me.

"Did she leave a forwarding address?"

She snorts. "Not with me." She waddles away, and I sink down on the steps.

She's pregnant with my child, and I can't even speak to her. The pain that rips through my heart is unbearable. What I've wanted most, what I've dreamt about for the past five years—it's painfully out of reach. Every time I think I might be happy, every time I think I might have a wife, a child, a *meaning* to this miserable existence, it's snatched away from me. I look up at the sky and start laughing as tears roll down my eyes.

Karma is beautifully vicious, isn't it?

I'm paying for my crime a thousand times over. When Brianne was taken away from me, I made the biggest mistake of my life, and someone lost their life because of it.

Then, Nicole was dangled in front of me like an irresistible lure, and I fell for her, *hard*. I fell so hard I don't think I'll ever be able to get up again. She was everything that I lost, and more. She was my second chance at love, at a family, at everything that I'd lost. She was more than that. She understood me in ways I thought weren't possible. She fit into me so perfectly that it felt like we were made from the same mold.

And I lost her, too.

I laugh until my chest hurts, and I lie back on the steps. Puffy white clouds pass across the sky, oblivious to my pain.

I squeeze my eyes shut and shake my head.

I don't want to go to jail. Tears prickle at my eyelids when I think of turning myself in to the police. I'd be disbarred, convicted, charged, and I'd lose everything.

What help would that be?

Nicole would have my child, and I'd be behind bars. Our kid wouldn't stand a chance.

No, I can't do that. I might have turned myself in to the police before, but the baby changes everything. I have to make sure that Nicole is taken care of.

There has to be another way. I take a deep breath and try to organize my thoughts.

I committed a crime. I'm guilty. I treated Nicole like shit, and I didn't come clean to her when I should have. Now, she's no closer to getting closure and she's carrying my child.

Pain radiates from my heart and I groan. Money was tight

enough for her before, and now there's a baby in the mix? Paralegal salaries aren't exactly amazing. How can she think she can do it on her own? Why didn't she tell me?

But I know why she didn't tell me. It's because she wants nothing to do with me, and I don't blame her. In a way, I admire her. Even with the shock of a pregnancy, she still won't sacrifice her morals. I imagine her back straight, her chin high, and that defiant glare in her eyes that I loved from the first day I saw her.

That's Nicole.

My Nicole.

I stare at my phone, and I know I can't do anything. She shut me out a month ago.

An idea springs into my mind as I think of Nicole's life insurance policy. Knowing what I know about insurance companies, they're still stalling.

She'd sent me the information to pass on to my friend who specializes in insurance law, so I look up the email. My heart thumps when I see her name in my inbox, and I take a deep breath.

This is my chance.

Maybe not for her to take me back, but for me to make things right. This is my chance to atone.

I can't help Nicole and the baby by being in jail, but I may be able to provide for them in another way. Even if she never speaks to me again, the least I can do is make sure the mother of my child is safe.

33

NICOLE

I TOSS the stack of mail onto the counter, along with my purse, keys, and phone. I'm starving. I don't know if it's the pregnancy, or work, or the fact that I went swimming tonight, but I feel like my stomach is a bottomless pit.

I have some leftover spaghetti sauce, so I set a pot of water to boil and grab some hummus and carrots to munch on while I wait. I inhale a few carrots and my stomach groans happily. With some food in my belly, I'm functional again. I turn to the stack of mail and sigh. At least most of it is making it to my new address, so the mail forwarding service is working properly.

Bills, bills, and more bills. That's all it is. How depressing. Oh, and another delay letter from my insurance company. Great. My life is just so joyous. I moved into this shoebox apartment three weeks ago, when I realized that I could no longer afford my slightly-bigger-shoebox apartment.

Like I said, joyous.

I consider throwing the insurance envelope directly in the trash, but then I sigh.

I work in the legal field. I know that I need to keep all the records that the insurance company sends to me. If I ever get enough money to put together a claim against them, it'll make it easier to argue my case.

So, popping another carrot in my mouth, I tear the envelope open. I unfold the letter with a sigh, already knowing exactly what it's going to say.

Except... it doesn't say what I think it's going to say.

I stumble backward, clutching my chest. I inhale a piece of half-chewed carrot and start choking on it. I cough and splutter, turning toward the sink and hacking until the half-masticated carrot comes up. My eyes are streaming with tears and my heart is racing. I lean against the sink, breathing heavily.

"Sorry, baby," I say, whispering to my stomach. "That was scary, wasn't it?"

I rub my belly, soothing my unborn child. Yesterday, the OB-GYN told me it was as big as a raspberry. I take a deep breath and see the offending letter on the ground where I dropped it.

Gingerly, I pick it up with the tips of my fingers. There's nothing in my mouth to choke on, but I sit down on a chair just to be safe. I read the letter again.

Dear Ms. Nicole Martinez,

We are pleased to inform you that your claim on Policy Number 6579326 with regards to the Deceased Jack Martinez has been approved. Payment in the amount of $1,000,000.00 will be deposited into the account nominated below within five to ten business days.

My eyes skim over the bank details and I read the letter over again. My heart beats faster and I close my eyes. I clutch the letter to my heart, putting a hand to my stomach. *A million dollars!* I knew that was the amount I was entitled to for Jack's life insurance, but as the months dragged on, I didn't believe I would actually get it.

I'd started feeling ridiculous for even thinking that I'd get that kind of money.

But now...

"Hey, little Raspberry," I say to my baby. "We're going to be okay." I smile, and then laugh, and then read the letter again.

My medical debt will be paid off. My baby will have a college fund. I won't have to stay in this shitty one-bedroom apartment. I can get a new car. A *new* car! I've never in my life had a brand-new car!

I have a chance.

I cry, and laugh, and read the letter until I hear the pot of water boiling. I'm too excited to eat, so I just take the pot of water off the stove and grab my phone.

"Jenna," I say, breathless. "You'll never guess what just happened. The insurance came through!"

My sister squeals over the phone. I can imagine her jumping up and down. Her kids laugh in the background.

"You hear that, kids? Auntie Nicole just got some very good news! And you're going to have a very healthy, happy little cousin!"

I laugh, reading the letter one more time just to be sure.

"How?" Jenna breathes. "How did this finally happen?"

"I don't know. Maybe they finally realized they had to."

"Did you ever get a lawyer to pressure them?"

"I can hardly afford my membership at the YMCA," I laugh. "He-who-shall-not-be-named was supposed to get his lawyer friend on it, but that all went out the window, obviously. I may work with lawyers but I can't afford them."

"Surely you get an employee discount or something."

I laugh. "It doesn't matter anymore. Oh my gosh, Jenna, I didn't think it would actually happen! I was starting to panic. You know, the baby, and being alone, and..."

"Well, this will take a load off your mind."

"I think I'll still keep working until the baby comes." I stare at the peeling wallpaper in the kitchen, smiling. "I don't know what I'd do with myself otherwise."

"Do whatever you need to do, little sister," she says. I can hear her smiling over the phone. "Any chance you want to come over for dinner?"

"I'd love to." My heart does a backflip and I start laughing again. "I'm having trouble focusing right now. I can't even manage to boil some water for pasta."

"Well, the kids are eating now, but I'll keep your plate in the oven."

"Be over in ten minutes."

I hang up the phone and I can't keep the smile off my face. It's not just the money that's making me feel this way, it's the relief. All the stress of providing for myself and my baby. All the bills and debts that have been adding up over the past year and a half. All the things that I've had to give up—my car, my apartment, my special lattes on the way to work—I won't have to worry about that anymore. My baby will be able to go to college! I'll be out of debt! I'll be able to *buy a house!*

Like a crazy person, I laugh and laugh by myself. I rub my stomach and do a little dance in my kitchen.

It's just money, but it's life-changing. They say money can't buy you happiness, but right now, I feel pretty darn happy. Life just got a whole lot less stressful.

It's September, and the weather is starting to get colder, so I wrap myself in a jacket and head for the bus stop. Then I smile and shake my head. I can afford a cab now. I go back up to my warm apartment and call a taxi. While I wait, I sit back on my couch with my hands over my stomach.

"Everything is going to be okay," I tell my baby. "It's all going to work out."

For the first time in months, I see that light at the end of the tunnel that Jenna told me about. There's a glimmer of hope for me, a chance for me to be stable and happy.

My thoughts drift to Martin, but I stop myself. I won't let his memory tarnish what otherwise has been a happy evening.

Maybe, when the payment comes through, I'll work up the courage to tell him about the baby. Then I won't feel like I'm asking him for money or begging him to support me. I can go to him with my head held high, and then he can choose whether or not he wants to be a part of the baby's life.

My heart squeezes at the thought of seeing him, and I take a deep breath. I owe it to my child to have its father in our lives. As painful as it may be for me to see him and talk to him, I need to think about what's best for my baby.

But that's something for Future Nicole to deal with. Right now, I'm going to go be with my sister—with my family—and I'm going to be happy.

34

MARTIN

It's been a week since the insurance company accepted my offer. They've given me thirty days to honor my end of the deal, which means my life is about to change drastically. The sun has just gone down, and I flick the lights on in my living room. Most of this stuff will have to be sold before I get rid of the apartment.

I frown when I hear a knock on the door. I'm not expecting anyone, and I don't like surprises. When I open the door, Carmen gives me a smile and holds up a bottle of whiskey.

"Drink?"

"I, uh... sure."

I let her in, confused. She's not exactly one to make house calls.

"You miss me already, Carmen?" I ask, grinning as I lead her to the kitchen. She slides onto one of the bar stools at the island, pushing the bottle of whiskey to the middle.

"Maybe I do."

"It's only been a few days since I left the firm. It's not like you to drink on a Tuesday night."

"How do you know how often I drink?"

"Fair point," I chuckle. I put two tumblers on the countertop and drop an ice cube in each. "So... what's up?"

Carmen nods as I pour her drink. She takes a sip, staring at the amber liquid and sighing.

"Are you sure about your decision?"

"To quit? Yes. Carmen, you can't protect me. If this whole mess were to get out, imagine what it would do to the firm. It's better for me to leave quietly."

"I just don't understand why you had to do it like that. Why wouldn't you just let me help you?"

I sigh, staring out into the starry night. "I've been running from my problems for long enough. It's time for me to face them."

"Is this you trying to get back together with Nicole? You make sure she gets her insurance payout and then she'll love you again?"

I laugh, knocking back the whiskey. It burns as it travels down my throat, and I pour myself another glass. I shake my head.

"No, I'm not trying to win her back. I'm pretty sure that ship has sailed."

"It just doesn't make sense, Marty. You're such a bright lawyer. You're throwing everything away."

"Not my integrity. And I'm still a lawyer."

My former boss stares at me, shaking her head.

"What changed?"

I lean against the counter and stare at a spot on the floor. I haven't told anyone about the baby—it seems wrong. That should be Nicole's news to share, not mine. She probably doesn't even want me to know.

So, instead of telling Carmen the truth, I just shrug.

"It just became too hard to keep it a secret anymore. I killed a man, Carmen. And I can defend it with all the excuses in the world. I can talk about Brianne, and the baby, and the icy roads, but at the end of the day, I did it. I hit them, and I didn't stop. I could have been the difference between him living and dying. I'm the reason she's been in physical therapy for a year and a half." I poke my chest. "Me. I need to face that."

"You could go to prison, Martin," she says quietly.

I shrug. "I think I've prevented that."

"How? Even you're not *that* good a lawyer."

I laugh, arching my eyebrows. "You don't think so?"

She narrows her eyes and takes a sip of whiskey. "What are you up to?"

I chuckle and shake my head. "Nothing. I haven't done anything wrong. I called Nicole's insurance company and struck a deal."

"What kind of deal?"

"Why are you so interested in this, Carmen?"

She sighs, staring at me and shaking her head. She takes another sip and stares out the window and after a few moments, she finally speaks.

"I'm interested because I don't think you're thinking straight. You're not fit to be making these kinds of decisions."

"I disagree, this is the clearest my mind has been in over a year and a half, maybe even longer."

She stares at me, and I know she doesn't believe me. Why would she? A few weeks ago, she was breaking the law to protect me. Then, I did a one-eighty and decided to quit. I know Carmen, and I know that she's not going to let this go unless I tell her the truth.

Plus, that's kind of my new thing—telling the truth.

I take a deep breath.

"I knew Nicole's insurance company from when we were together. I'd seen the forms. So, I called them, and I struck a deal."

"You said that." She narrows her eyes. Her lips form a thin line and she shakes her head. "What *kind* of deal, Marty?"

"I told them I'd pay the full amount of the life insurance policy if they agreed not to press charges or pursue me in any way. I had them sign an NDA. It's watertight."

Carmen's eyes widen. "You're paying out of pocket?"

I nod.

"How much was the policy?"

"It was enough," I shrug. I glance around my apartment, knowing that I'll have to sell it in the next few weeks. Paying a million dollars out of pocket will nearly wipe me out completely. All my assets, my cars, my savings, most of my stock portfolio.

I'm going broke, but I'm doing the right thing.

"Jesus Christ, Marty. And you quit, too? How are you going to support yourself? I mean, I get this whole noble gentleman thing you've got going on, but you have to think about yourself, too!"

"I've done enough of that lately."

Carmen sighs. She drains her glass and stares at me. "You're sure about this?"

"Yeah."

"And you don't want to keep your job?"

"Look, Carmen, I'm flattered. Working for you has been the best experience of my life. I care about the firm more than I can say, and that's why I can't keep working for you. No matter how watertight the NDA is, I can't risk this coming back on you."

"I never knew you were so selfless."

"I wasn't."

Carmen looks me in the eye, and finally extends her hand toward me. "Well, if I can't convince you to come back to work, I guess I have to let you go. Good luck, Martin."

"And good luck to you, Carmen."

She shakes my hand, and then gathers her bag.

"You want your whiskey?" I say, picking up the bottle.

Carmen laughs. "I think you need it more than I do."

I grin and walk her to the door. With a sigh, she puts her arms around me and gives me a hug. It's the most intimate thing that Carmen has ever done. It's weird, but nice. My eyes start to prickle with emotion and I pull away, clearing my throat and blinking rapidly.

"Alright, you idiot," she says. "Don't come begging me for a job in six months' time."

"I won't." I grin, but I'm not exactly sure it's true.

"If you did, I might actually have to take you back." She smiles sadly, and then nods. I turn the doorknob and open the door, and then take a step back in shock.

"Nicole!"

She's standing in front of my door with her arm raised, ready to knock. Her eyes flick from me to Carmen and back again.

"Hi, sorry," she stammers. "Is this a bad time? I'm sorry, I'll go."

She turns to leave and I reach out to catch her hand. "No, wait! Stay. Carmen was just—"

"I was just leaving. Good luck, Martin. My door is always open."

I nod to Carmen, who slips past us and walks away without looking back. Nicole pulls her hand out of mine and my heart sinks.

"I... you want to come in?"

She swallows. Her big, dark eyes look terrified. She straightens her shoulders and nods.

“Sure.”

35

NICOLE

AS SOON AS the door closes behind me, my heart starts to beat harder. I think I've made a mistake by coming here. This is where he told me that he was the one who hit Jack and me. This is where my world shattered. This is where he put this baby in my belly.

Sensing my nervousness, Martin tries to smile.

"Tea? Coffee? Water? Whisk—no, I guess you can't drink."

I frown. "What do you mean?"

"Because you're—" His eyes widen. Martin bites his lip and clears his throat. "So, tea? I was just going to have some."

I glance at the bottle of whiskey on the counter, and I wonder what Carmen was doing here. Then, my mind circles back to his comment.

"What did you mean, I can't drink?"

He fills the kettle with water and then sighs. His back is to me, and I see his shoulders sink. When he turns around, his eyes are deep, blue wells of sadness.

"Stella told me about the baby."

My jaw drops, and anger floods my veins. "What?"

"I tried to call you and email you and I even went to your house, but—"

"I moved. When did she tell you?"

"Maybe two weeks ago?"

"Wow. Seems like I can't trust anyone." Bitterness leaves a bad taste in my mouth, and I walk over to the couch. I sit down, suddenly exhausted. "So, I guess there's no reason for me to be here, then. You already know."

"Don't be mad at Stella, please," Martin says. "She was doing it for you."

"Yeah," I say, staring out the window. He really does have a gorgeous view. I shake my head. "It's just hard to trust people when they do things like that."

Martin turns on the kettle and comes to sit across from me. He clasps his hands in front of him, resting his elbows on his knees. He takes a deep breath.

"So..."

"I'm not here to ask for money," I blurt out. His eyebrows shoot up, and his surprise makes me angry. Is that the only reason he thinks I'm here? I take a deep breath and continue. I had a whole speech planned out, but now that he already knows that I'm pregnant, I have to come up with something else. My heart is hammering, and my palms feel sweaty, and Martin is just as good-looking as ever, and I hate myself for thinking that.

"I want to do what's best for the baby, and I think having its father in the picture is the best thing. Now, if you don't want to—"

"I do. I want to." He leans forward, and my heart skips a beat. His eyes look so earnest it's hard not to believe him. But the walls I've built around my heart hold strong, and I swallow back the hope and desire and love that I once felt for him.

"Okay. Well, I moved, but I can unblock your number, and—"

"You blocked my number?"

"Can you blame me?"

He chews his lip, shaking his head. "No, I guess not." He looks like he wants to say something, but he holds back.

I take a deep breath and keep talking. My prepared speech is in shambles.

"Anyways, I'll unblock your number. Then, once the baby is born, we can arrange visitations. You've already met Stella, obviously, but she'll be representing me."

His face twists, but he nods. "Okay."

"Okay." I put my hands on my knees and get up. I nod to him and start heading for the front door. The kettle starts boiling as I pass the kitchen and I hold back tears.

"Nicole," Martin says behind me. I turn to look at him and see him run his fingers through his hair. He shifts his weight from foot to foot and finally takes a deep breath. "Thank you."

My eyebrows arch. I was expecting profuse apologies that I would be able to disdainfully reject. I was expecting my bitterness to grow, but with two little words, he's softened my heart.

Damn him.

I nod. "Yeah. Okay."

"I'm going to be moving, so I'll send you my new address."

"Oh, upgrading from this dump, huh?" I say, sweeping my arm around his luxury apartment. "Is that what you and Carmen were celebrating?"

He laughs, shaking his head. "No. Nothing like that. Pretty much the opposite. I quit, and she was trying to convince me to change my mind."

"You quit?" I frown. That's not like him. His job was everything to him. "Did you get a better offer somewhere?"

He laughs again. "No. I..." He takes a deep breath, and once again I feel him holding back from me. "It was just time to go."

"Oh."

He stares at me with those pain-filled eyes of his and purses his lips. He swallows and then nods, and steps forward to open the door for me.

"I'll send you my new address when I have it," he says.

"And I'll unblock your phone number."

He nods. We stand awkwardly until I finally clear my throat and walk through the door. Everything in my being screams at me to stop and turn back toward him, but I don't let myself. I put one foot in front of the other and walk down the hallway until I'm out of sight. Then, I hear his door close, and I break down in tears.

Jenna is waiting for me outside. She gets out of her car and wraps her arms around me, saying sweet, motherly things into my ear as I sob.

"I'm proud of you, Nic," she whispers. "You did the right thing. You set boundaries. You're so strong, little sister."

"I don't feel strong right now," I sob. I snort and wipe my nose on my sleeve, sighing.

"You are. You're going to be the best mother in the world."

I nod and let her guide me to the car. When we drive away, I steal one last glance at Martin's building before hardening my heart against him a little bit more.

That was infinitely harder than I thought it would be, even with all the mental preparation I'd done. He's just so... *him*. He's so handsome, and sexy, even when I hate him. And today, he was so kind. I was expecting him to be shocked about the baby, and maybe to tell me he wanted nothing to do with me. I thought he'd tell me to get rid of it. I thought I'd have a fight on my hands.

Instead, he *wanted* it. He wanted me!

I cry silent tears as Jenna takes me home, finally pulling myself together as we drive onto my street. I look at the little run-down building and sigh, shaking my head.

"Thank goodness for that insurance pay out."

"What a blessing," Jenna says with a sigh. She squeezes my hand and smiles at me. "I'm proud of you, Nic. Everything is going to work out just fine."

"Yeah," I say, nodding. "Okay."

36

MARTIN

By the time my thirty days are up, I've sold my apartment and my car, and I've paid the insurance company. All those bonuses were good for something, in the end. I move into a small apartment in the city, and I start looking for a job.

My communication with Nicole is minimal, but at least she answers my texts now. I try to give her some space. When she came to see me, I saw how difficult it was for her.

I'm still coming to terms with how deeply I hurt her. The hope that I have of ever winning her trust is slowly dying, but I know that all I can do is show her that I'm a different man.

A couple weeks later, I take a job as a public defender. The offices are cramped and understaffed, and the budget is tight. I have six times as many cases as I had at Sanders & Perry, and less resources to fight them with. Still, there's a buzz in the office that didn't exist before. Clients aren't ranked based on the size of their retainer. I'm surprised to say that I actually enjoy it.

The void inside me starts to slowly heal. My work

becomes purposeful. I'm not chasing dollars, or wins, or reputation anymore. I'm chasing justice. I'm working myself to the bone and it feels good.

The first time I see Nicole since that night at my apartment is when we decide to have lunch together. When I ask her out, I don't expect her to say yes. When she does, I end up smiling like an idiot for the rest of the day.

A few days later, she walks into the Public Defender's offices and takes my breath away. Her hair is thick and shiny, tumbling around her shoulders. Her baby bump is starting to show and my heart skips a beat.

Fear curls in my heart when I see her. My thoughts jump to Brianne, and all the trauma and heartache that surrounded her pregnancy. But Nicole just smiles at me and hitches her purse higher on her shoulder.

"You ready?"

"Yep," I say, shuffling a few papers and locking my office door. She looks around and smiles at me.

"This is different. I never would have imagined you working in an office that wasn't entirely made of glass and pretentiousness."

I laugh, putting my hand on her back to guide her down the steps to the sidewalk. I pull my hand away, clearing my throat. It still feels so natural to be beside her.

"I'm actually really enjoying it. There's a lot more energy in the office than there was at Sanders & Perry. Maybe everyone is just overworked," I grin.

"Maybe. I'm happy for you." She smiles at me, and a bolt of lightning passes through my chest. How does she do that? All these weeks, I thought I was getting over her. I focused on work, and on moving, and on rebuilding myself from the ground up.

I thought that my feelings for her would fade, but they've

only gotten stronger. I open the door to the cafe for her, and we find a table near the window. I get us a couple menus and sit down, smiling at her.

"So how far along are you now?"

"Twenty weeks. I'm getting so big!"

"You're beautiful."

She blushes, burying her face in the menu. My heart skips a beat, and I look down at the menu without reading it. My whole body is buzzing. I haven't been this close to her in weeks, and I don't know how to act. I steal another glance at her, and in that moment, I *know*.

I know that she's the one for me. She's the only one I'll ever love, no matter how I try to get over her. She's the mother of my child, and the love of my life. No matter what I do, from now on, it'll be for her and for our baby. She may never accept me, she may never trust me, but I'll be there for her.

Maybe this is my penance for all the wrong that I've done. It'll be my lifelong torture, to know that the woman I love is painfully out of reach.

Still, it's the sweetest torture of all. She tucks a strand of dark hair behind her ear and I know that there's nowhere I'd rather be.

I'll spend my life trying to win back her trust. Even if I never do, I'll be here. I need to be. There's no other way that my life can go on.

Nicole catches me looking at her, and I glance back down at the menu.

"The Cajun chicken sandwich looks good," she says.

"Yeah," I reply. I still haven't been able to actually read any of the words on the menu. My heart thumps, and I watch as Nicole bites her lower lip.

I would kill to kiss her right now. My hands are itching to

run through her hair, and to pull her body next to mine. I glance at her bump, and I wish I could run my hand over it. What would it be like to feel our baby kicking?

The waitress comes to take our order, and I just tell her I'll have the same thing as Nicole. I can't focus. Nicole smiles at me.

"You look good," she says. "Like... clearer. I don't know. Your eyes aren't so sad."

I smile. "I have sad eyes?"

"You used to."

"I was living a lie."

Her face falls, and I regret saying it. She clears her throat, and her tone changes. It's all business now, and she discusses the arrangements for the baby. When I'll be able to visit, how much time I'll have with the baby, where she wants to send it to school when it's older, that kind of thing.

"Do you know if it's a boy or a girl?"

She shakes her head. "I think I'm going to wait to find out."

"That's very old-school of you. How will you know what color to paint the nursery?"

"I don't believe in gendered colors." Her eyebrow arches. "I'll paint it like a rainbow."

"Is it safe for you to be breathing in paint fumes? Maybe I could paint it for you."

"I'll hire someone," she says, glancing out the window. Her hands twist into each other, and I know I've overstepped a boundary. I take a deep breath. I don't want to mess this up. This is the first time I've seen her, and she's still fragile. I need to be here for her, and for the baby.

If that means being patient with her, then I can do that. If that means being celibate forever, then I guess I can do that too.

When I see her eyes light up as our food hits the table, I know I'll never be able to be with another woman. I just hope that she'll forgive me one day. When we walk back to the office, the tension between us has eased the tiniest bit. When we say goodbye, Nicole smiles and kisses my cheek.

I watch her walk away with a big, dumb grin plastered across my face.

37

NICOLE

"IT JUST KICKED!' My eyes widen, and I put my hand on my stomach. I reach for Stella's hand and put it on my stomach. "Can you feel it?"

"That's amazing," she laughs. She puts her other hand on my belly and giggles. "That feels so weird!"

"She's strong!"

"Is it a girl? I thought you were waiting to find out."

"I am. I just think it's a little girl," I laugh. "I could be wrong."

Just then, the conference door opens. Carmen and a young lawyer from Sanders & Perry walk through the door. Her eyebrows raise in recognition and she nods to me.

"Nicole."

"Carmen," I say. "Hi. I didn't know you'd be here today."

"This is an important case. Should we get to work?"

All business, all the time. That's Carmen. I take notes throughout the meeting, trying not to stare at her. She looks exactly the same. She's just as intimidating as she was when I worked for her.

When the meeting is over, I chase Carmen toward the elevators.

"Carmen!" I say. "Carmen!"

She turns around, her eyebrows arched in surprise. "Is everything okay?'

"Yeah, everything is fine," I say. I glance at the lawyer with her and nod to pull her aside. The little jog from the conference room to the elevators has rendered me out of breath. I inhale, finally able to speak. Her eyes flick to the hand on my stomach, and her eyebrow arches.

"I just wanted to say thank you for everything. I was such a mess when I left Sanders & Perry, I don't think I properly thanked you for the opportunities you gave me."

Carmen's eyes soften and she puts her hand on my forearm. "You were a great employee, and I was sad to see you go. The firm has changed a lot, since you and Martin left." She shakes her head, sighing. "I understand why he did what he did, with the insurance company, but I still don't think he had to leave."

I frown. "The insurance company?"

Carmen's eyes widen. "He didn't tell you?"

"Tell me what?"

"I thought that's why you were at his place, that evening."

"Tell me what, Carmen?" My voice is harder, and my whole body starts to shake. Carmen looks away from me. She clears her throat.

"I should go."

"Carmen!"

"I shouldn't have said anything. Fuck," she breathes. "Martin has always been my weakness, ever since he came to me as an arrogant young lawyer fresh out of law school. I shouldn't have said anything. I'm sorry, Nicole. You're going to have to ask him."

"What did he do? Is that why he quit?"

She nods. "He said he wanted to protect the firm, but I've always thought he wanted to protect you, you know, in case anything came out in the press. He didn't want you to be at the center of any controversy." She shakes her head. "He'd never admit that, obviously. But that's just what I think."

My breath is ragged. My head is spinning. I don't know what to think. Carmen smiles at me sadly, shaking her head.

"He's crazy about you, Nicole."

"He's not. He doesn't care about me." My voice is shaking and weak, and Carmen just sighs. She nods to her coworker, who's staring at his phone by the elevators.

"I should go."

I want to stop her and force her to tell me what's going on. I want to pull her back and make her tell me the whole story, but my feet stay rooted to the ground and my voice stays silent. I watch her get into the elevator and disappear, and then I lean against the wall and sigh.

The insurance? What did Martin have to do with the insurance? I put my hand to my head and try to take deep, calming breaths. Panicking won't be good for the baby.

Her words swirl around my head, knocking loose all the things that I've tried to ignore. All the feelings that I have for Martin come surging back up inside me, and my defenses weaken. I turn to see Stella watching me, and she nods.

"Go."

My lip trembles, and I nod back. I speed-walk to the elevator and mash the button until the door opens. Then it's a blur of waddling, taxis, and heavy breathing until I get to Martin's offices.

"I'm here to see Martin Henderson." I'm breathless, and sweaty, and I probably look like a crazy person.

"Do you have an appointment?"

"No, but—"

"I'm sorry, ma'am, you're going to need an appointment."

"Listen, just call him and tell him Nicole is here to see him."

"He's asked not to be disturbed."

I put my knuckles on the desk and take a deep breath. "I guarantee you, he'll want to talk to me."

I tap my fingers on the reception desk as the lady phones his extensions. I listen to her say my name, and I pace up and down until she tells me I can go through. Her eyebrow arches and she watches me walk by. I ignore her.

Martin is waiting for me at the door to his office. His eyebrows are drawn together and he looks at my face, and then my stomach.

"What's wrong? Is everything okay? Is the baby okay? Nicole?"

"The baby's fine," I say, brushing past him into his office. I plant my hands on my hips and spin toward him. He closes the door, watching me.

His arms hang by his sides and his face is blank. The air between us is thick with everything we've left unsaid. I want to scream. I want to hurl his stapler at his head and I want to melt into his arms and kiss him. I can't think straight.

Finally, I take a deep breath.

"What happened with Jack's life insurance?"

His eyebrows arch and he looks away from me. "I don't know." His shoulder hitches up slightly. "What do you mean?"

"Martin." My voice is hard. I take a step toward him.

He glances at me and takes a deep breath. "I don't know what you're talking about, Nicole."

"Carmen told me."

His eyes widen and then he lets out a deep sigh. "Fuck. She told you?"

I nod. He stares at me, frowning.

"What did she tell you?"

I sigh. "Martin! Just tell me the truth! Isn't that your new 'thing'? The truth? Tell me what happened. Don't I have a right to know?"

My legs tremble. I hate pleading with him. I hate the fact that once again, he's holding all the cards. He rakes his fingers through his hair and makes it stand on end. He motions to a chair and sits in the one across from it.

I lower myself down, putting a protective hand over my stomach. Martin takes a deep breath.

"I made a deal with the insurance company. I confessed to them, and told them I would cover the policy if they agreed not to press charges and signed a non-disclosure agreement."

My jaw drops. I stare at him, unmoving.

"I didn't want to tell you, Nicole. I didn't want you to think... I don't know what I was thinking. I didn't want you to think it was charity, or me trying to get back in your good graces. I just wanted to do the right thing. The fewer people that know, the better. This would be exactly the type of thing that the press would pounce on. When Stella told me about the baby..." He sighs and shake his head.

"You did this for the baby?"

His eyes flick up to mine. They look like crushed velvet—full of pleading and pain and something softer. "And you."

"You gave up your whole life for us?"

Laughing, he shakes his head. "I didn't give anything up, Nicole—only money. I thought I gave up a lot, but working here... it's good. And I've gotten to see you." He stares out the window and shakes his head. "I just needed to know that you'd be okay. I just wanted to do the right thing for once in my miserable life."

Tears start streaming down my face as I stare at him. He wrings his hands together, staring at the floor between us. His hair is standing on end, and his tie is crooked. His shirt is partially untucked and he has big, purple bags under his eyes.

He looks like a mess, and he's never looked better.

He's a mess because he cares about me. He's a mess because he cares about the baby. He changed his whole life, gave up everything he cared about, just to make sure our baby was okay.

He didn't even tell me.

I push myself up and close the distance between us. I run my fingers through his hair and pull him toward me. He exhales slowly, resting his head against my stomach. His hands come up to my bump, and we both start quietly crying.

My tears fall onto his thick brown hair as I hold him close to me. His hands stroke my stomach, my waist, my back, and a flame of desire ignites inside me. My heart flutters, and the defenses I've built around it dissolve into nothing.

Martin looks up at me as tears stream down his face. He wraps his arms around my waist and kisses my belly before looking back up.

"Nicole, I'm sorry. I'm so, so sorry for everything. I never want to hurt you again, and if you don't want me in your life, I understand. I'll always be here for you. I still love you with everything I have, which isn't much, but—"

"Shut up, you big idiot," I say, sobbing and laughing. I lean down and press my lips to his. He pulls me closer, running his strong, broad hands up under my shirt. He moans as he deepens the kiss.

I yelp and laugh as he picks me up and lays me across his

lap. Tangling his fingers into my hair, he presses his forehead to mine.

"You're the love of my life, Nicole. I hope you'll forgive me one day."

"I just did." I kiss the tip of his nose and let out a long sigh. "I've missed you."

"You have no idea." He shakes his head, staring deep in my eyes. I hook my arms around his neck and take a deep, cleansing breath.

When he kisses me again, his lips are soft, and his touch is tender. He lays a hand on my stomach and sighs. We hold each other for a few long, quiet moments. For the first time in months, I'm truly, completely content.

38

MARTIN

HOLDING Nicole in my arms is making my heart palpitate in dangerous ways. I run my hands through her hair and pull her close to me. We sit in my office for a long moment, together.

She came back to me. She wants me.

She forgives me.

I didn't think it would feel like this. I'd resigned myself to seeing her from a distance, to being satisfied with the minimal contact that she allowed.

But now...

Now there's real hope! I have a chance!

I run my hand up and down her spine and she groans. I kiss her again, softly, and then she pulls away.

"Martin..."

My heart falls. I try to keep my face steady.

"Yeah?"

"I just..." Her breath hitches. "I want to take it slow."

"Of course."

"I feel like I can't trust you."

"You can."

She sighs. The sadness in her eyes is unbearable. She cups her hand on my cheek and stares deep in my eyes. Her eyes are shining silver today, and the green specs are bright.

"It's a lot to take in."

She disentangles herself from me and stands up, smoothing her pencil skirt. Her baby bump is showing more and more every day, and all I want to do is put my hands on it and kiss it and talk to it.

But I don't.

I watch her smooth her hair and take a deep breath.

"Have you gotten a new car yet?"

She shakes her head.

"Not yet. I'm trying to be responsible and do lots of research. The insurance money seems like a lot right now but I have to be smart or it'll be gone in a flash."

Hope takes hold in my heart. "At least let me drive you back to work."

Her lips twitch, and she dips her chin down. "Okay."

Sitting next to her in the car is torture, and I love every minute of it. We don't speak. After a few minutes, Nicole turns on the radio. Adele comes on over the speakers and Nicole quickly switches the channel. I glance at her, grinning.

"I've been crying to that song for weeks." She sucks her bottom lip between her teeth, then starts laughing. "I'm sick of it now."

My heart squeezes. I did that to her.

We drive the rest of the way in silence. When I drop her outside the office, every muscle in my body is screaming at me to lean over and kiss her, but I know I can't. I watch her gather her things and give me that little half-smile.

"See you later, I guess." She tucks a strand of hair behind her ear.

"I can drive you home," I blurt. I don't want this to end.

"It'll be more comfortable than the subway, in your condition."

"In my condition?" Her eyebrow arches.

My lips drop open. "No, I... I didn't mean.... I just..."

She laughs, then, and an arrow goes through my heart. That's the laugh I fell in love with. Her eyes glimmer. She grins at me, shaking her head.

"I'll text you when I'm finishing up."

My heart does another cartwheel. I nod.

"See you tonight." I watch her walk into the building. When she gets inside, she glances over her shoulder at me. Her lips twitch, and I don't think I've ever been happier in my life.

She wants me. I know she does. She wants to love me, to be with me, to let me hold her in my arms.

She wants the same things I do.

I take a deep breath and start driving back toward my office. No matter how long it takes, I'll wait for her. I'll show her that I'm not the same man I was before. I'll drive her home every single day if that's what it takes. I'll paint the nursery and help her carry her shopping bags.

I'll be there.

I'll show her what she means to me. I'll show her that no one else matters except her and the baby.

With renewed resolve, and hope burning a little bit hotter in my heart, I let myself smile. I smile all afternoon and smile harder when she texts me. I smile when she gets in my car and try to keep a straight face as we drive in silence.

I walk her to her door, and she nods at me.

"Thank you, Martin."

"Same time tomorrow?"

Her lips quirk and her eyes search my face. "What's your angle, here?"

"My angle is making sure you're comfortable and safe and home every evening."

She stares at me for a few moments and finally chuckles. "Okay." And then she disappears through the front door. I stare at the door for a few seconds and put my palm against it. It stays well and truly closed, but I don't care.

I'll come here every day for as long as it takes.

Nicole is mine, and I'm hers. I don't want anyone else, or anything else, except her and our child and our life together.

For the past couple months, I've been in a deep, dark hole. I've come to terms with my mistakes and punished myself a thousand times. I've given up my career, the one thing that has kept me going. I've gone bankrupt.

It means nothing, though, compared to Nicole's smile. I'd give up my career a thousand times, go bankrupt over and over and over again just to see that glimmer in her eye.

I turn around and walk back to my car. I glance once more at the building, at the closed door, and I take a deep breath.

Every. Single. Day.

I'll be here as long as she lets me. I'll get her home safe, and make sure she's comfortable. I'll drive her to her doctor's appointments if she lets me.

Whatever it takes, and as long as it takes, I'll be here.

I get back in my car and glance at the apartment building one more time. The curtains on the second floor move, and a smile twitches at my lips. She's there. She kissed me. She's given me hope.

From the moment I saw her in that parking lot, she was meant to be mine.

Now, I'm going to prove it to her.

39

NICOLE

Two months later...

The elevator door dings open and I step out, smiling. Martin stands up from the benches in the lobby and extends an arm toward me.

"Hey, beautiful."

"Hey, Big Shot."

He grins. "How was work?"

I tell him about my day as he leads me to his car. Ever since that day in his office, he's picked me up from work every day. He said he didn't like me taking the bus home, and I haven't gotten around to buying a new car.

I haven't admitted it to him, but I've been stalling on the new car. These moments with him are the best part of my day.

We've taken things slow. My heart is still fragile, and I haven't wanted to jump into anything. When I told him that, after we kissed in his office, I thought he'd be angry. I thought he'd be mad or try to convince me. Instead, he just nodded. He respected my wishes. He listened to me.

Now, when I slip my hand into his, I know I'm ready. I'm

ready to be with him. I'm ready to end his torture. I'm ready to wrap my arms and legs around him and tell him that I'm his. I'm ready to run my fingers through his hair and see the joy in his eyes when he feels our baby kicking.

I'm ready—so ready it makes my heart want to explode.

He opens his car door for me and I get in, watching him jog around the front to get in the driver's seat.

My heart thumps as he drives me home. When we pull up outside, he smiles at me.

"You look beautiful."

"Do you want to come up?"

His eyebrows shoot up toward his hairline. "Yeah. Fuck yeah! Yes." He clears his throat. "I mean, yeah, you know, whatever."

I laugh, smacking his arm. "Come on, you goon."

He puts his hand on my lower back when I fumble with my keys. I'm still in my shoebox apartment, but not for long. Soon, the baby and I will have our very own house.

When we walk in, I nod to the boxes I've started packing.

"I'm moving to the new place next week. I've never owned a house before." I smile, looking at the boxes. Martin slips his hand around my waist and kisses my temple.

"You deserve it."

I spin in his arms, putting my hand on his chest.

"Thank you for waiting for me. I know I've been distant. I just..." I sigh. "Just... Thanks."

He shakes his head, laughing softly. "Nicole, I would wait my entire life for you. I would drive you home every single day, rain or shine. I would do anything."

He rests his forehead against mine. "You have to understand that nothing else even comes close to the way I feel about you."

My heart does a backflip and butterflies explode in my

stomach. Sensing my excitement, our baby starts to kick. I grab his hand and put it on my stomach. His eyes light up and a delighted smile breaks over his face.

"Wow."

It's the first time I've let him do that. I've seen the way he looks at my stomach, and how his hands twitch when I touch my bump. It's been too intimate to let him touch it.

Now, it feels right.

With his hand on my stomach, and my chest so close to his, desire starts to flame inside me. I drag my eyes up to his face, licking my lips. Martin watches me, letting his hand drift up my stomach. He brushes his hand over my breast and I sigh.

"Nicole," he growls.

"Yes?"

I run my fingers up his chest, hooking them around his neck. He groans as I press my body against his. His hands run to my back and down to my ass. He squeezes it, resting his forehead against mine.

"I want you," he breathes.

"Even when I'm a giant pregnant whale?"

"You're not a whale," he laughs. "But yes. Pregnant, not pregnant, it doesn't matter. Always. Everywhere." He squeezes my ass again and desire sparks in my veins. Instead of answering, I tilt my chin up and press my lips to his.

At first, it's tentative. As soon as I part my lips and feel his tongue diving into me, I'm done. I moan, curling my fingers into his hair. My nipples harden and I press my whole body against his. His hands slide down my thighs, and without warning, he picks me up. I wrap my legs around his waist, giggling.

"You sure you can carry me? I'm heavier than before."

"I'm sure," he laughs. We kiss and I squeeze my legs

around his waist. My skirt rides up and I grind my center toward him. The space between my legs grows hotter, and my need for him grows.

Because that's what it is—a need. I don't want him. I *need* him. I need his kiss, and his hands, and his cock. I need his mouth on my body and I need his voice in my ear. I need his breath to wash over my skin and I need his scent all over me.

I need him.

"Bedroom," he says between kisses, his hands cupping my ass. He spreads my ass cheeks apart and I moan. I can feel his cock, rock hard between us.

I nod toward the bedroom and he carries me toward it. When he lays me down on the bed, he sighs. I watch as he unbuttons my shirt and slides it off my shoulders. He slips my skirt off and groans. I'm not exactly wearing sexy underwear, but he looks at me like I'm a Victoria's Secret model. Caging me against the bed, he kisses me hard. His hand drifts to my breast, my side, my ass.

Unhooking my bra, he tosses it aside. When his lips connect with my breast, I gasp. It's like my nipple has a direct line to my center. He licks and nips and kisses my breast, toying with my other nipple with his hand. I'm panting, curling my fingers into his hair. I feel like I'm going to come just from that. He kicks my legs apart and slips his fingers under my panties.

"So fucking wet," he groans as he slides his hand up and down my slit.

"For you," I pant.

He slides two fingers inside me and I moan. I arch my back, letting my legs fall open. He curls his fingers just right, kissing my neck and whispering everything and anything into my ear. I don't hear him. I don't understand. All I can focus on is the pleasure burning between my legs.

Just when I think my orgasm will crash into me, he slips his fingers out of me. He tears my underwear down my legs and groans.

When he flips me over, I yelp.

"On all fours," he commands. I do as he says, my breasts and belly hanging down as I prop myself up on my elbows and knees. He spreads my legs apart, his hands drifting from my knees to the backs of my thighs. He spreads my ass apart and sighs.

When his tongue connects with my slit, I gasp. His hand twirls around my clit as his tongue finds my opening. He doesn't just lick me, he *fucks* me with his tongue. In and out, he fucks me with his mouth, his tongue, his fingers. His hands drift to my ass and he spreads it wide, sliding his tongue up to my ass.

I gasp, feeling dirty and bad and so fucking good. His tongue slides around my ass and then gently inside. My legs shake and I grip the blanket. My whole body is on fire. The pads of his fingers find my clit again, and his tongue keeps working my ass. When he slips his thumb inside my opening, I scream.

I scream his name, I scream *oh god*, I scream *yes*, I scream wordless moans as my whole body shakes. Martin moans with me, fucking my ass and my pussy and my clit until my orgasm is dripping out of me.

He licks up every drop, groaning.

"I've been dreaming of that for months." I look over my shoulder at him with hooded eyes. I can't even speak. I watch him tear off his shirt and unbuckle his pants.

He kicks them off in an instant, and I just stay there, recovering. I'm still on my elbows and knees, with my forehead resting on the pillow. I just need a breath. Just a second to recover. Just—

He drives his cock inside my quivering pussy and I gasp. He's so hard, so hot, so fucking good. My fingers curl into the covers as my back arches for him. I push myself back onto his cock and moan.

When he smacks my ass, I sigh. The pleasure he gives me is indescribable. He drives his cock deep inside me until another orgasm washes over me, and then a third.

I collapse. My legs can't support me anymore. He lifts my ass up and fucks me harder, pushing my hair off my back. He leans down, his face near my ear.

"I'm going to come," he grunts.

"Come, Martin," I gasp. "Come inside me."

He grunts, moans, and explodes inside me. I feel every pump, every drop, every throb, and I love every second of it.

When we fall apart, I watch him catch his breath. His hand falls toward me and I interlace my fingers in his. He turns his head toward me and sighs.

"I love you so fucking much, Nicole."

My heart explodes. I nod. "I know."

"I'm never going to let you go."

"I don't want you to."

He smiles, turning toward me. He drapes his arm over my body and pulls me in for a deep, tender kiss. We intertwine our arms and legs and lay in a sweaty, happy, post-orgasmic heap.

I run my fingers through his hair and smile.

"I love you too, Martin."

He grins, his eyes sparkling. "I know."

EPILOGUE

MARTIN

Five months later...

Our baby girl's cries are the most beautiful sound I've ever heard in my life. Nicole is crying, laying back in the hospital bed as a nurse drops our baby on her bare chest.

"Skin to skin contact is important," she says. "Hold your baby for a few minutes. Congratulations, you two."

Nicole's hands stroke our baby's tiny back as tears stream down her face. She glances at me, smiling through her tears. I put my hand on our baby's head and my eyes mist with tears.

This is the happiest day of my life.

There have been so many happy days that it's hard to rank them, but seeing our baby for the first time makes my whole world just a little bit brighter.

Nicole strokes the baby and kisses its head. The baby is wrinkly with a big bald patch on the side of her head, but she's perfect.

"I love you," I say, kissing Nicole's forehead. I stroke her hair, pushing it off her sweaty forehead. She smiles at me. "You were incredible. I'm glad I'm not a woman."

Her eyes are hooded with happiness and tiredness and

the incredible glow of a mother. I wrap my arms around my two girls and my heart beats for them.

"Martin," Nicole says softly.

"Hmm?"

"I have a name in mind for her."

I lift my head up and stare at Nicole. Her eyebrows are arched, and she bites her lip.

"I'm not sure you'll like it."

"What is it?"

We haven't talked about names. I just moved into the house last month, and we've been busy getting things ready. With both of us working, and a new house to get organized, there hasn't been much down time. It feels like this moment right now is the first time we've been able to catch our breath.

Nicole looks at the baby girl and joy shines on her face.

"Jacqueline Brianne Henderson."

My heart thumps. My eyes mist. I find Nicole's hand and interlace my fingers in hers. I squeeze her hand as a tear rolls down my cheek.

"You would be okay with that?" My voice is choked with emotion. Nicole is so beautiful, inside and out. So many women wouldn't want to be reminded of Brianne.

Not Nicole.

Nicole runs head-first into the memories, into the grief, and she shines her beautiful light on all the sadness. She obliterates all the badness around her. She's completely, utterly *good*. Her goodness heals me, strengthens me, teaches me what it means to be compassionate and caring.

"It's perfect," I say. "Jacqueline Brianne Henderson."

"I was worried you wouldn't like it."

"I love it." I kiss Jacqueline's head and my chest feels so good it almost hurts. "And I love you."

She smiles at me, and I fumble in my pocket. When my

fingers touch the little velvet box, I suddenly feel nervous. What if she says no?

This is a ridiculous time to propose to her. I should have done something more romantic—something big. A grand gesture to show her what she means to me.

But then, Nicole slides her hand over my cheek and I know that this is perfect. She wouldn't want something big. She just wants honest, true love.

So, I pull the ring box out of my pocket and flip it open.

"Make me the happiest man in the world, Nic," I breathe. My voice is choked with emotion.

Her eyes widen and tears start falling again. Her breath hitches and a laugh tumbles out of her. She nods, closing her mouth and nodding harder as the tears spill down her cheeks.

"Is that a yes?"

"It's a yes, Martin. It's a yes," she laughs. I take the ring and slip it over her finger. She watches it catch the light and then nuzzles against our baby girl's head.

"You hear that, Jacquie? You daddy's going to make an honest woman out of me."

The nurse comes to swaddle the baby and take her away to be cleaned up and checked. I watch her go and then wrap my arms around Nicole. She shifts in bed, and I climb onto the tiny single hospital bed beside her. With my arms around her, and her head resting against my chest, I feel like the luckiest man alive.

She looks at the ring and I kiss the top of her head.

"You're wrong, you know." I rub my hands up and down her arm.

"About what?"

"I didn't make an honest woman out of you. You're the one who made an honest man out of me."

She turns to me, smiling. Her hand slides up my cheek and I kiss the woman of my dreams, the mother of my child, the love of my life.

~

Thank you for reading!

If you'd like access to the Lilian Monroe Freebie Central, which includes bonus chapters from all my books (including this one), just follow the URL below:

http://www.lilianmonroe.com/subscribe

Lilian
xox

Psst.. keep reading for a preview of Book 2: Loathe at First Sight

LOATHE AT FIRST SIGHT

LOVE/HATE: BOOK 2

1

ASHLEY

I WASN'T EXPECTING Police Chief White to knock on my door. I try to keep my face steady as a cold current crawls down my spine. He's gained a bit of weight since last year—the stress of the job, no doubt. His wobbling jowls dip down in greeting.

"Mrs. Thompson," he says, taking his hat off and smoothing his hair.

"It's King," I answer automatically. I never took my husband's name, but that didn't prevent anyone from calling me Ashley Thompson from the moment we said our vows. Randy never corrected anyone. I think he resented me not taking his name.

Police Chief White opens his mouth and closes it again. "Ms. King," he mumbles. He shifts his weight from foot to foot as I tighten my grip on the doorknob.

Last time I saw him, he was handing me a folded American flag and the Denver Police Department Medal of Valor. I was in a haze of grief, relief and confusion after my husband had been shot in the line of duty.

Now, the Chief stands before me again in full uniform, and the memories of that day start to flood my brain.

"May I come in?"

My hand squeezes on the doorknob as I try to steady myself. I swallow past the lump in my throat and nod, opening the door wider to let him in.

Police Chief White's boots thump on my old wooden floors as he makes his way inside. He's at least six inches taller than me, towering over everything in my cramped old house. His eyes glance around the room as he stands stiffly.

"Please," I say. My voice is strangled as I motion to the couch. He nods and takes a seat. "Coffee? Tea?"

"No, thank you," he says. "I just came here to give you my condolences. Today is one year since—"

"I know what today is."

"Right." He clears his throat. He won't meet my eye as he thumbs the edge of his hat. "I wanted you to know that you still have the full support of the DPD behind you. Losing Superintendent Thompson is still something the department feels every day. And I'm sure the past year has been... difficult for you."

I sit down across from him and smooth my hands over my legs. "Thank you."

I can't look at him. I can't look him in the eye and keep pretending I'm sad that the man who abused me for years is now dead. I pretended enough last year. I went through the wake and the funeral, through the awards ceremonies and the newspaper articles about how brave and valiant and *good* my late husband was.

He wasn't.

He was a violent, jealous, angry man. He was vengeful, and he had a short fuse.

And somehow, he hid it from everyone. Even me. It wasn't until we were married that the mask started to crack. The first time he hit me was our one year anniversary. When that happened, I was ready to leave him. I had my bags packed and one foot out the door.

Then the tears started, and the apologies, and the promises that he'd never do it again. He was ashamed of himself, he said. He'd never do it again, he promised. He was tender and loving; he was the man that I'd married.

And then he did it again, and he apologized again.

He did it over and over, until he broke me. I was a shell of my former self.

Then, Randy Thompson was shot and killed. He was a hero, but I was still the same battered woman.

White shifts in his seat, and I drag my eyes up to meet his. He's staring at me with the detached suspicion that police officers always seem to have.

He clears his throat. "Your husband was a good man, Mrs. Th—Ms. King. His loss is felt in the department every day. I just wanted to personally come here and make sure that you have everything you need. I know today may be tough for you."

The big man wrings his hands. He clears his throat, and I finally take mercy on him and end his torture by responding.

"That was very thoughtful of you, Police Chief Wh—

"Please, call me Charlie."

I smile. "Charlie. Thank you very much. It's been a tough year, but I'm getting through it. I appreciate everything you've done for me since Randy died."

"Of course." He heaves himself off the sofa and stands awkwardly in front of me, as if he's not sure whether to hug me.

Please don't hug me.

"Well," he huffs, nodding. He puts his hat back on his head. "Have a great day, Ms. King. And let me know if you need anything."

We both breathe a sigh of relief as he turns toward the front door. His duty is done, and I won't have to pretend anymore. The sooner he's out of my house, the better.

It's not that I don't appreciate the visit—I do. He doesn't have to come visit me. A lesser man would forget about the wives of their fallen men. The police chief is a good person.

I know that, but I'm just sick of pretending.

Every time I meet someone who knew Randy, I have to keep up appearances. Even from the grave, Randy is controlling me.

I'm sick of it.

The police chief's boots thud on the creaky floors, and he finally reaches the front door. This will be over soon, and I'll be able to focus on my work. I'll be able to forget about Charlie White, about Randy, and about that horrible day one year ago.

But when he opens it up, another man is standing there with his finger heading for the doorbell.

"Oh!" The man's dark eyebrows arch upward. "Police Chief White! I wasn't expecting—"

"Councilor Maguire." The chief's face darkens, and he brushes past the man without another word. The man stares after him, jaw hanging open.

I take the few seconds to look him up and down. He's a good-looking man, with a well-tailored suit. His hair is parted on the side and perfectly styled. His fingernails are clean, and his shoes are polished. When he turns back toward me, he smiles genially. He has a dimple on his left cheek.

"Good afternoon, Ma'am. My name is Adrian Maguire." The name rings a bell. I nod. His teeth are perfect. "I've been a city councilor in our fine city for the past six years, and I'm running for mayor in the upcoming elections. I wanted to take the opportunity to introduce myself."

He smiles a bit wider, but it doesn't quite reach his eyes. He extends his hand toward me and we shake firmly.

"I'm Ashley King."

"Ashley." He hasn't stopped smiling, and I wonder if his cheeks hurt. "Can I ask, how do you know the police chief?"

Adrian Maguire has a way of making you feel comfortable—he's mayoral. I'm not sure he's sincere, but then again, he's in politics. Sincerity isn't part of the job description.

"Well," I say, considering not answering his question. More talk of Randy's death means accepting more unnecessary condolences.

But in a way, I want to know how Councilor Maguire will handle it. I want to see how good his poker face really is.

I smile sadly. "My husband died a year ago today—he was on duty at the time. The police chief was offering his condolences."

"Well, let me offer mine as well," Mr. Maguire says without missing a beat. "Is it safe to say that safer streets would be high on your list of priorities?"

I smile inwardly. *Smooth.*

"Why, are you going to be 'tough on crime'?" I ask, arching an eyebrow. I've heard that one before—what politician *hasn't* used that line?

Mr. Maguire smiles. "I won't feed you bullshit lines, Ms. King. You probably know more than most about the inner workings of law enforcement. I can promise you that I'll do everything in my power to make sure that police officers are safe. We want to make sure that what happened to your husband doesn't happen to any other serving police officer."

"That's all anyone can ask for."

I try to smile. I'm growing tired of this conversation. It's the same as the conversation I had with Police Chief White—it's all platitudes and fluff. There's no substance, no truth. I want to close the door and retreat to my living room where I won't have to pretend.

"May I ask if you'd be willing to vote for me in the upcoming election?"

"It'll take more than one conversation to secure this vote, Councilor Maguire," I grin. "Now if you'll excuse me, I've got dinner on the stove, and..."

"Of course. Here." He hands me some pamphlets, and I watch him leave before closing the door.

I don't actually have any dinner on the stove. I've been thinking of getting comfortable with a spoon and a jar of Nutella tonight. The jar of Nutella sounds even more appealing right now than it did fifteen minutes ago.

My phone dings from the coffee table, and I walk over to look at it

Reminder: Denver Construction Awards
Tomorrow, 7pm

I work as the Media Relations Manager for one of the largest construction companies in Denver. We're up for a couple of awards, so tomorrow night will be important. Hansen Constructions is trying to bid on some major projects in Denver, so upping our image is very important right now.

That's why they hired me.

But right now, thoughts of the police, of Randy, of the election are swirling in my mind. I had a hard week at work, and the last thing I want to think about is the unpaid overtime I'll be doing at this awards ceremony. I swipe the reminder away and head for the Nutella before collapsing on the couch. I flick on the TV and try to stop my whirling brain.

One year.

It's been one year since Randy was shot. One year since *it* happened. One year since the nightmare that was my marriage ended.

One year since I got out.

And frustratingly, it's taken me almost a year to forgive myself. Not for what happened the day he died—I'm not sorry about that—but to forgive myself for letting him do those things to me. I'm just starting to feel like myself again, to open my eyes and realize that my life isn't over.

With every threat, every insult, every slap, every punch, every burn, Randy tore at the fibers of my identity. He unraveled me, thread by thread, until I was nothing but a tangled heap on the floor. And then he stood over me and laughed.

Everything that I thought I was—strong, independent, loveable—he took it away from me.

Maybe naively, I thought his death would give that back to me. I thought I'd be myself again.

It didn't. I'm not.

A part of me grieved. It surprised me and confused me when I felt sad. He was my husband, and we'd been married for seven years. But a bigger part of me wanted to close that chapter of my life and move on. The sadness was more confusing than the anger or the relief.

I stare into the jar of Nutella and take a deep breath. Something shakes loose in my chest and I stare vacantly at the TV screen.

It's time for me to move on. I can't pretend anymore.

I want to be free. Free from him, and free from the memories of what happened, free from the past.

One year later, I'm stronger. I've landed on my feet. I'm alone, but I'm surviving. I'm more than surviving! I'm *thriving*. I have a good job, something that Randy never allowed me to pursue. I'm reconnecting with my friends, and I've even started playing music again.

For the first time since I married Randy Thompson, I feel hopeful about the future.

Maybe I'll even be able to date again. Anytime a man has tried to come near me, I retreat into myself again. But now... I think I'm ready. Some men are good—I just happened to be fooled by one of the bad ones.

I dig another spoonful of chocolatey hazelnut spread out of the jar and eat it slowly, sighing.

The police chief's visit rattled me. Just when I think I'm done with Randy, someone shows up on my doorstep to remind me of all the mistakes I've made.

There's one mistake that I'll never admit to. I'll take it to the grave with me—no matter what. I did what I did, and Randy got what he deserved.

And now, it's time to move on.

2

LIAM

CAMERAS FLASH as I put on my brightest smile. I adjust my athletic shorts and jump from one foot to the other. Music is blasting at the start line, with the announcer calling out the beginning of the race. It's only a matter of seconds before the first annual Heart Start Race begins.

I never thought it would get this big. We have over twenty thousand entrants for our first year, and we've been able to raise close to half a million dollars from the race alone. As long as today goes well, it'll be a huge success for the foundation.

It'll be a huge success for me.

At least it would be, if I cared. I'm just doing this until my brother wins the election, and then I'll be done with this bullshit charity work.

As another camera flashes in my face and I do my best to look happy and confident, the worry knots in my stomach.

Ten miles.

It's not a huge run. Six years ago, I would have been able to manage it easily. But now, six years and one heart surgery later, and ten miles feels like a run to the end of the earth.

I used to run ten miles multiple times a month. My longer runs were a compliment to the intense training I did for my main event: the 800m run. Middle distances had always been my favorite, even as a child. It is, in my humble opinion, the most challenging distance in any track meet—it's too long for an all-out sprint, like the 100m, but too short to settle into an endurance pace.

It's two minutes of hell. Or if you're like me and you've made it to the Olympics, it's just shy of two minutes of hell. But after those two minutes, I got to stand on that podium with a solid gold medal between my teeth, and I was on top of the world.

Click, flash, smile. Another photo.

The announcer's voice booms over the speakers and he starts to count down.

"Three... two... one..."

A gunshot sounds and the mass of humanity around me starts to move. Men and women in bright spandex start to run along the designated route. I watch people pass me with their running belts strapped with water bottles, energy gels, and snacks.

Others have nothing, just old running shoes and the race bib pinned to their free t-shirt.

I'm trying to take it easy. Ever since I had my operation, my heart hasn't felt the same. If I push myself too hard, I get light-headed and my pulse goes through the roof.

I've been cleared to run for months now, and I've worked up from short walks to now being able to participate in this race.

It should be a celebration. I should be happy. Running in my own foundation's race is a milestone I wasn't sure I'd be able to achieve.

I'm an Olympic medalist who was told he might never run again, but here I am.

I won.

I'm a champion.

I beat the heart defect. I beat the surgery. I beat the odds.

But as mothers with their strollers, children, and even toddlers start to surround me, I don't feel like I'm winning at all.

I'm *slow*.

Victory isn't the point of this race, but I still feel like a failure. I was an Olympic champion! Now, I feel old and useless. I'm only thirty years old, but I feel closer to death than when I was on the operating table.

I know there are cameras everywhere, so I do my best to smile and talk to the runners around me. One young mother jogs beside me, pushing a stroller. She's wearing a tight purple running top and a matching hat.

"Beautiful day," I say to her, smiling.

She blushes, and I grin.

Maybe being at the back of the pack isn't so bad. I'd rather be surrounded by young, fit MILFs than the serious lanky runners at the front of the pack. At least back here, I have something nice to look at.

That's what I keep telling myself, anyway.

My heart trembles and my smile fades. I nod to her and slow down, running on my own again. A tremor in my chest always sends fear pumping through my entire body. I put one foot in front of the other, trying to keep the worry from creasing my forehead.

Nobody wants a picture of Liam Maguire collapsing at his own fucking race—especially not me or my family. This is supposed to boost my brother's campaign. We're presenting a united front, as my mother keeps reminding me. Then she usually says something about the cost of my heart surgery to remind me how much I owe her and my father.

I had an atrial septal defect—a hole in my heart.

But I could have told anyone that a long time ago. I used to think I had a hole where my heart should have been. I've never cared about love or relationships or matters of the heart. I've never cared about anything except running and winning.

And then that was taken away from me.

So, here I am. Running a ten miler for the first time in six years, gracing the back of the pack with a big, dumb fucking smile on my face.

When I'm sure that I won't drop dead in the middle of the race, I pick up the pace again.

There are bands playing on the side of the road, and big banners from our sponsors. My name is plastered everywhere. People are lining up on the side of the street, and I stop for a minute to take a picture with them. A woman thrusts her baby into my arms, and I smile for the selfie.

This is what I've been reduced to.

I'm not winning anything. I'm just a poster boy for heart defects.

A teenage boy with tears in his eyes sticks out his hand. I shake it.

"What's your name, buddy?"

"Nolan," he beams. His face is pale and he's leaning against a man who looks like his father. "I wanted to say—" he wheezes. "I have a septal defect, too. I hope I can run in this race next year." He wavers on his feet, and his father catches him.

A lump forms in my throat, and once again I feel like a fraud.

Who am I to give hope to these people? This poor kid

might be dead next week, and he's looking at me like I'm some kind of hero.

I'm not a fucking hero. All I did was survive. I was just lucky that my family is filthy rich, and I could afford the best medical care this country has to offer. I'm a product of my upbringing, through and through. This kid is, too, but he's on the other end of the spectrum.

He doesn't have billionaire parents and a trust fund to pay for a team of world-class doctors. I pat him on the shoulder. "You'll beat it," I lie.

I give Nolan my card and tell him to email me, and then I keep running.

After a torturous hour and a bit, I finally make it to the finish line. There are more cameras, more sponsors, more cheers and celebrations of my wonderful achievement of putting one foot in front of the other. This race wasn't my idea. My mother and father put me in charge of this foundation, and my brother has leaned on it ever since the start of his mayoral campaign.

We're one, happy, big-hearted family. We give back. We're pillars of the community.

... We're frauds.

And the biggest fraud of them all is me.

I don't care about these people. I don't care about fundraising or running this foundation. I don't care about the thousands of babies that die of congenital heart defects.

I don't even care about this race.

All I care about is the fact that I'll never get the chance to win another medal in my life. If I could trade all this fundraising, all the praise and the accolades for one more shot at an Olympic medal, I would.

All the good that this foundation is doing for people like Nolan—I'd trade that in a heartbeat.

Maybe that makes me selfish. Maybe that makes me the asshole who's still hanging onto the past. Maybe it makes me a heartless bastard.

Like I said, I always knew I had a hole in my heart. I don't think the surgery fixed me up completely. It patched up the heart in my chest, but it couldn't change who I am.

My brother greets me at the finish line with his posse of campaign staffers. They're carrying his placards, wearing wide smiles and pins that say 'Adrian Maguire: My Mayor'.

Adrian claps me on the back and turns me toward the cameras. He always knows where to find the photo opportunity. And once again, I look like the sick, weak brother as he props me up.

Once again, they'll talk about my heart defect instead of talking about me.

Tragic. A waste of talent. So brave.

I can see the headlines already.

My brother squeezes my shoulder and leans in toward me. "Well done, little brother."

"You owe me one."

"The press is lapping this up."

"You'd better win this election, Aido."

He squeezes my shoulder again and turns us toward another mass of reporters. His smile is unwavering, and his stupid little dimple is angled perfectly toward the cameras. I take a deep breath and do my best to smile with him.

Yes, he definitely owes me one. This whole thing—the foundation, the run, the fucking holier-than-thou Good Samaritan Mother Theresa bullshit that he has me doing—it better help him win this election.

And once it does, I'm going to bury myself in drugs, alcohol, and pussy until I forget the word 'Olympics' even exists.

~

Get Loathe at First Sight by copying this URL into your browser:

www.amazon.com/dp/B07RJT66H9

Don't forget to sign up for my newsletter to gain access to the Lilian Monroe Freebie Central:

http://www.lilianmonroe.com/subscribe

Lilian
xox

ALSO BY LILIAN MONROE

For all books, visit:

www.lilianmonroe.com

Brother's Best Friend Romance

Shouldn't Want You

Military Romance

His Vow

His Oath

His Word

The Complete Protector Series

Enemies to Lovers Romance

Hate at First Sight

Loathe at First Sight

Despise at First Sight

Secret Baby Romance:

Knocked Up by the CEO

Knocked Up by the Single Dad

Knocked Up... Again!

Knocked Up By the Billionaire's Son

The Complete Knocked Up Series

Knocked Up by Prince Charming

Knocked Up by Prince Dashing

Knocked Up by Prince Gallant

Knocked Up by the Broken Prince

Knocked Up by the Wicked Prince

Knocked Up by the Wrong Prince

Fake Engagement/ Fake Marriage Romance:

Engaged to Mr. Right

Engaged to Mr. Wrong

Engaged to Mr. Perfect

Mr Right: The Complete Fake Engagement Series

Mountain Man Romance:

Lie to Me

Swear to Me

Run to Me

The Complete Clarke Brothers Series

Extra-Steamy Rock Star Romance:

Garrett

Maddox

Carter

The Complete Rock Hard Series

Sexy Doctors:

Doctor O

Doctor D

Doctor L

The Complete Doctor's Orders Series

Time Travel Romance:

The Cause

A little something different:

Second Chance: A Rockstar Romance in North Korea

Printed in Great Britain
by Amazon